The Fields of Clon Miarth

This book is a work of fiction. Any resemblance to actual events or persons, living or dead, is entirely coincidental.

"The Fields of Clon Miarth," by Samuel Schiller. ISBN 978-1-60264-054-2.

Library of Congress Control Number on file with Publisher.

Manufactured in the United States of America.

The Fields of Clon Miarth

Samuel Schiller

To my friend, NancyJane Langford,
whose enthusiasm and gentle nature
have been my inspiration.

Other books in this series:
Warrior of the Son (Book One)
Priests of Moloch (Book Two)

Artwork by Laurie Gowland

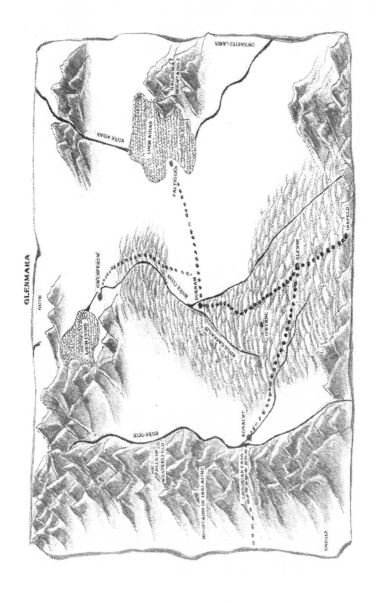

CHAPTER I
SIEGE

Death birds darkened the skies over Durham. They converged on the eminence of the Sceir Naid and before the sun had reached its zenith, they covered the battlements, rooftops and spires overlooking the palace yard. There, scattered across the blood-darkened cobblestones, a grisly feast awaited them.

The dead and dying littered the marble steps, and sprawled together in a tangle of torn flesh beneath the gateway arch. Slaughter stained the polished floors of the Great Hall and spread throughout the palace corridors. Even in the cathedral, among the sacred symbols of the One True God and His Risen Son, a horror of blood gave mute testimony to the terrible battle that had raged for control of the kingdom. But the treachery of Moloch's priests and influential Glenmaran nobles had been thwarted for the moment, and in the aftermath, High King Osric Murchadha met with his retainers.

They were few. The young, ambitious Duke Morleigh Dunroon, the older, more cautious Duke Eiolowen, and the truly aged Duke Fardoragh, made up the higher nobility in Osric's camp. An oddment of dignitaries and merchants joined an assortment of Barons and a collection of knights and men-at-arms. The remnant of the Red Guard and the Palace Watch made up the balance of the five hundred souls loyal to their king.

Beyond the high crenellated walls that separated the fortress from the town, the soldiers of Duke Robert Fitzwarren took control of the city with an efficiency that contrasted their failure to seize the palace. Together with Duke Broderick Laighan, the would-be usurpers commanded a force that outnumbered Osric's own by more than five to one. But for the time being, they couldn't get into the palace.

Osric pushed his unkempt brown hair from his weary brown eyes. Exhaustion etched harsh lines across his face, battering his spirit in kind with his body. Not an hour before he had been bound to the cathedral altar as a sacrifice to the dark power of Moloch. Then in a miracle that defied any explanation but the intervention of Almighty God, his brother, Evan MacKeth, crippled and ill, drove the priests and soldiers from the church and saved Osric's life. From that moment until this, there had been no time for reflection, and there was precious little time for it now, but he had just received news every bit as dire and disturbing as anything that had already occurred. Aine Ceallaigh, the sister of his Queen and Evan's intended, had been taken.

The details were wrung from the unfortunate Guthrum Fitzwarren.

"What was your part in this?" demanded Osric of the cringing, wounded prisoner.

"I had no part in anything, Majesty! I followed my brothers, that's all. I didn't know what they were doing!"

"Very well. Strap him to the table."

Strong hands pulled Guthrum from his chair and dragged him across the room.

"Wait! Wait! Sweet mercy, don't! We were only supposed to open the gate. I didn't want to harm anyone. My brothers attacked Lord Halfdane, not I."

"Your cowardice isn't in question. Now tell me of Aine Ceallaigh. Where is she? Be quick."

"She stabbed me with an arrow!" Guthrum protested, but when Osric stepped closer he quickly added, "Eowulf took her. He was following Claranides and those priests. They're going to the Hinnom Valley. That's all I know. I swear!"

"How many men does your father have? Who else is part of this treason? Give me numbers and names, or upon my oath I'll strip the flesh from your bones!"

Information poured out in a trembling torrent.

Now that the interrogation was over, Osric considered the paradox of the man who had thwarted the plans of Aelfric, Eowulf and Guthrum: Anwend Halfdane. From the fjords of Varangia across half a continent he had come to this desperate moment. He stood at the window now, slumped shoulders further diminishing his slight stature until he looked tired and old. His coarse grey hair, partially hidden by an untidy, blood soaked bandage added to the impression of weakness and infirmity, but without his valiant defense of the palace gate, the kingdom would have been lost.

"It's rumored you have some knowledge of fortifications," Osric offered.

Anwend turned a battered face toward the king. "It is true, majesty," he replied.

"Perhaps you might suggest where the enemy will attack."

Anwend approached the table and pointed with a callused finger. "Unless they're complete fools, they'll concentrate here," he said, indicating the main gate. "It's the weakest point."

Duke Dunroon snorted and rolled his steel-grey eyes. "Gates usually are."

"Especially this one," returned the Varangian with equal sarcasm. "I've seen better gates protecting vegetable gardens."

"What's wrong with the gate?" asked Osric.

"It's falling apart. The drawbridge can't be raised without the whole thing coming down, and it won't take them long to realize it. But there's a solution if your majesty would care to hear it." Heated discussion followed.

"They'll come through the tunnel in the church," argued Dunroon.

"It's too easily defended. They'll go for the gate."

"If they set a fire in that tunnel they'll collapse the whole fortress wall."

Anwend shook his head and stamped his foot on the marble floor. "There's solid rock beneath us. You'd never crack this hill. But I think I know where that tunnel begins."

"Indeed?"

"Just beyond the wall is a house with a copper roof. There were a great many people going into that house last night, and none of them came back out."

"You amaze me," marveled Osric. "Sit with us Lord Halfdane."

The planning continued.

In the corner of the room, Evan MacKeth muttered through clenched teeth, his green eyes swollen and red from tears. Rust-brown patches of dried blood dulled his armor, matted his auburn hair and spotted his beardless face. Though his heart still beat, and he yet drew breath, it was as though he had died the moment he discovered Aine was lost. He had nearly thrown himself into the river in a suicidal attempt to rescue her, but his companions had prevented him. Yet death in the river couldn't have been worse than the helplessness he was drowning in now. He began pacing the room, certain the despair in his heart would crush him if he didn't move. Nearby, Martin Reamon, a slight servant boy of fifteen, matched his master step for step.

Across the chamber, Brian Beollan, Aine's protector since she had been a young girl, sat alone and wept. He found neither power in his arms nor courage in his heart. He had failed, and now Aine was gone.

Shadow crowded the room despite the sunlight flooding through the high windows. At length the king went out to the wall beside the gate.

——— — — ———

The world was dark and still and quiet until the pounding began. In the distant shadow a drumbeat of pain insinuated itself into the silence, growing and expanding until it erupted into the waking world of stark reality. Aine's head throbbed and her stomach knotted in savage unease. But then someone gently cradled her head and placed something cool and wet over her eyes. She moaned.

"There, there Biscuit," said a familiar voice, "I'm sorry I had to hit you."

Aine stiffened as her mind filled with the terrible remembrance of her circumstance. She was in the brutal hands of Eowulf Fitzwarren.

"Relax," said Eowulf. "You'll feel better in a moment."

Her stomach heaved and she threw up, redoubling the pain in her head. When she was finished, Eowulf removed the wet cloth from her eyes and wiped her mouth. Now she could see.

Aine found herself in a woodland glade surrounded by towering oaks and bordered by a tiny, gurgling brook. It might have seemed picturesque in other circumstances.

Seated nearby, Phillipus Mauritius, the false priest, glanced at his companions. Aine returned his gaze, her eyes blazing with contempt as she recalled his deceit, his complicity in the treachery that had caused her dreadful predicament.

Eowulf loomed above her, his midnight hair framing dark, dangerous eyes. A trace of uncertainty flitted across the harsh features of his face as he dipped the cloth in the stream and wiped Aine's face. "Pretty Biscuit," he cooed and kissed her on the forehead.

Aine rounded on her captor, tried to strike him and scratch his face, but he grabbed her wrists and pulled her down.

"Don't touch me!" she hissed, a demand rather than a plea. "You will not touch me! Ever!"

"You're my prisoner," responded Eowulf as though trying to clarify their relationship, "so I suppose I've got to touch you."

He couldn't understand why she didn't welcome his tenderness. It had never worked for him as well as brute force, but seeing the cruel bruise beneath one bright blue eye, he wished he hadn't hit her so hard.

"You will not touch me," she warned. "Whatever you intend to do with me it will not include touching. Do you hear me Eowulf Fitzwarren?" She had no idea what was going to become of her, but she knew her captor didn't respond to suggestions.

"You have nothing to say about it," snarled Eowulf and a dangerous glint crept into his narrowed eyes.

The pounding behind Aine's eyes returned, diminishing thoughts of resistance, and she found she was very thirsty. Moreover, the truth of Eowulf's words rang loud in her ears. She didn't have much to say about it--at the moment.

"Water," she said, and lowered her head into her hands. Eowulf released her wrists, started to stroke her hair, but went to get water instead.

Aine's mind whirled. What was happening in Durham? Were her family and friends safe? What was going to happen to her? Were they really going to the Hinnom Valley? So many unanswered questions and her head hurt so devilishly! She drank a little water, lay down and closed her eyes.

"Get her up," said a voice. "I've brought horses." The warm flush of resurgent fear swept over Aine as Claranides, High Priest of Moloch came into the clearing. His was an iconic face, a visage so familiar that even after his banishment it was like seeing an old friend again, until one saw the eyes. Black, bottomless, they offered an uncomfortable view into a pitiless soul.

"She needs rest," offered Eowulf.

"Then stay. You're just a guest anyway. The rest of us are going to the Temple. Now."

Eowulf hesitated, the thought of returning to face his father flitting across his tormented mind. But the prospect of that happy reunion was too frightening to contemplate, especially since he had abandoned his brothers to the mercy of the king. Only slightly less terrifying was the thought of taking sanctuary with Claranides and his lot. He pulled the girl to her feet.

Moments later Aine found herself on the front of Eowulf's horse, galloping through the trees. Amidst the agony from the jolting ride she prayed for those she loved and for her own salvation. She couldn't know that her prayer had been answered even before it had formed in her mind. Everyone she loved had been saved by the valor of Evan MacKeth and Anwend Halfdane, and high above her, floating lazily in the warm morning sky, an angel of sorts was at that moment looking down on her.

———————

It didn't take long to get Duke Fitzwarren to the gate. Though reluctant to come face to face with the Monarch he had plotted to kill, once the summons had been sent, Fitzwarren came quickly.

From the battlements, Osric glared down at his treacherous vassal.

"What do you want?" snarled the Duke.

"First treason and now bad manners? How you disappoint me," Osric scolded.

"You won't think it so funny when we pull you down from your high place!"

"Pull away," encouraged the king, "But first let us speak of family matters." Soldiers pulled Aelfric and Guthrum to the parapet.

"Well?" queried the king.

"Well what?" howled the Duke. The defiance in his voice failed to conceal his frustration and dismay. His sons were treacherous creatures, worthless and without merit, but they were still his sons. "What do you hope to gain by this? Do you think I'll give up the crown?"

"The crown isn't yours to give up. Come take it if you may. And if you have nothing of value to barter for these two then I suggest you withdraw or I'll hang them."

"I'll not bargain with you. Don't waste time; you haven't much of it left!"

Osric hurried back to the hall. Duke Fitzwarren's failure to bargain for the release of his sons made it clear he didn't hold Aine Ceallaigh, confirming Guthrum's story. The King gave instructions and one by one his retainers left to do his bidding. Finally, only three remained: Brendan Ceallaigh, Duke Eiolowen and Evan MacKeth.

"My Lord Eiolowen," said the king, "Send someone to muster your retainers and the Faltigern Militia."

He turned to Baron Ceallaigh. "Find your daughter. Bring back our songbird."

Brendan's eyes brightened with gratitude. "I will stay with you, majesty," he asserted, "Brian Beollan will go in my stead."

"As you wish," Osric said, "And my brother will accompany him."

Evan's heart leapt. "But surely you need every sword you can get," he said. "I cannot leave you to the whims of fate."

"Our fate rests in God's hands. While we face our enemies here, three stout souls must seek their fate elsewhere."

"Four stout souls!" cried Martin. "My life for Lord Evan and Lady Aine!"

The Sceir Naid stirred with activity all that long, warm day. Provisions were carried into the towers for easy access. Sheaves of arrows and bundles of spears were disgorged from the armory and every able man and boy was armed for the coming struggle.

Out in town, furious efforts were made to seal off the palace fortifications from the outside world. Cavalry patrolled the banks of both rivers while the main of the besieging army took up positions in the town. The banners of Duke Laighan and Fitzwarren fluttered over the city.

At the king's direction, Anwend Halfdane began work on the gate. Given fifty men and all the small boys who could do heavy labor, he set them to stripping stones from the Cathedral courtyard wall.

The Four Stout Souls prepared. Duke Eiolowen tasked his nephew, Padraigh Rinn, with raising an army to break the siege. A formidable man, Padraigh remained silent and grim, which was to say he was no different than he always was. Brian Beollan stalked about the chamber as if searching for a victim to destroy. Indeed, to spill blood would have offered a perverse release to his overwrought emotions.

Disconsolate, Evan tried to dislodge the terrible visions filling his head: visions of little Aine dead, visions of the end of his whole world. As the afternoon wore on he withdrew to silent prayer.

Martin struggled with his own doubts. His boundless impetuosity had committed him to a dreadful adventure: swimming the treacherous River Cuinn and striking out across nearly a hundred miles of hostile country. Even if they managed to reach Faltigern, there was little hope of overtaking Claranides.

Could he keep up with three seasoned warriors? What if he slowed them down? Indeed, what if he drowned as seemed likely with his poor swimming skills? He shuddered, desperately wishing he might turn to Lord Evan for comfort and reassurance. But Evan was praying, and it seemed improper to interrupt.

The boy wanted to pray too, but found he didn't know how. What were the mechanics of it? Everything he understood about gods indicated that a priest was required as an intermediary. The average fellow couldn't talk directly to God. Yet somehow that was exactly what you were supposed to do with the One True God. It was quite confusing.

Still, this God, or as Evan put it, *the* God, had real power. Martin could see it even now in his restored master. He didn't know much about The One True God or Iosa Christus (If there was *one* God, why did there appear to be two?), but His power was undeniable.

"I'm sorry to interrupt while You're talking to my master," whispered Martin, "but . . . do You know how to swim?"

In mid afternoon a large entourage of horsemen approached the fortress gate. Accompanied by a great fanfare of trumpets, a herald demanded the king relinquish all rights, properties and authorities to Duke Robert Fitzwarren on pain of death. They received an immediate response.

Morleigh Dunroon vaulted to the top of the battlements and spat over the wall. "You will not address the king, you treasonous lot, nor shall he suffer to speak to the likes of you! You will end your days beyond the reach of the sun, weighed down by chains, gnawed upon by rats. Your masters have led you to your doom! Now begone, you pack of jumped up peasants. Your stench is beyond bearing!"

An arrow shattered on the parapet beside him, instantly followed by a swarm of missiles flying in both directions. Morleigh ducked behind the wall.

"You don't suppose I've angered them?" he asked.

Osric replied, "You have that way about you."

———

The exchange of words had barely ended when Fitzwarren launched an attack on the citadel. A thousand men charged out of the town, thrust ladders against the walls and began swarming up the battlements.

The defenders met them with a resolve that underscored their desperate position, and though a paltry number in comparison, atop the high, parapets of the Sceir Naid, their advantage was decisive. Yet despite the ladders that were pushed over or collapsed under the weight of men, weapons and armor, despite the men who fell to their deaths, or were killed by arrows and spears, greater numbers began to tilt the balance. The attackers gained the top of the wall.

Evan, Brian, and Padraigh threw themselves into the fray. There was no real skill required in such a fight; the ballet of steel Evan had learned long ago had no place in this battle. Here brute strength, desperate determination and merciless force matched itself against the same in a tangle of screams and carnage. The walls became choked with struggling, cursing men, who hacked, stabbed and tried to pry each other off the battlements. Blood poured from the wall walk gutters.

Elsewhere the assault broke down, though a steady exchange of archery continued. In the church an eruption of arrows from the tunnel drove the guards back and soldiers in the royal blazon of Broderick Laighan thrust up a ladder and swarmed into the room. But just as Anwend Halfdane had observed, it was a poor place to mount an attack. Before more than a handful had forced their inside they were overwhelmed. The survivors fled.

Once neither side could crowd any more men onto the wall, the battle degenerated into a great shoving match. The outcome was still in doubt when the arrival of a most horrible bird changed everything.

It dove down spouting fire, gnashing and slashing with razor honed teeth and dagger-like claws. Seeing one of their mates seized by the throat and thrown off the wall by this terrifying creature was too much for even the bravest attacker. But as difficult as it had been to climb the wall in the face of determined resistance, descending proved even more problematic. In the ensuing panic many of the attackers were cut down, forced screaming over the edge or jumped in a desperate, if fatal, attempt to save themselves. In a few moments it was over, and both sides paused to lick their wounds.

Evan collapsed beside the still twitching body of the last man he had killed. Brian rested against the blood-spattered stone, too weary to rise from the carnage befouling the wall walk. Padraigh howled a last invective at the retreating enemy, before he too slumped down.

"Warm work," he said between ragged breaths. "I'd give half of all I own for but the smell of water."

As if in answer to Padraigh's wish, Martin bounded up the steps with a bucket of water and a tin cup.

"You can make your fortune off this man," said Evan gesturing.

Martin's hands were shaking so badly that he nearly dropped the bucket. Padraigh seized it and helped himself. "What's wrong with you?"

Martin didn't answer. He had seen much pain and death in his short life; it was the way of the world. But nothing in his experience compared to what he had witnessed this dawn. The cries of the wounded, the awful rattling sound of men breathing their last, and the terrible effect of steel against the frailty of human flesh were overwhelming.

Evan pulled Martin down beside him. "Try not to think of it," he said, "There's nothing to be done. We didn't start this."

"I know, but it's all so awful, isn't it? And Lady Aine . . . my heart is broken."

"Stop whining like a suckling child," growled Padraigh, "and be about your business." He shoved the bucket back into Martin's arms.

"Listen to me Martin," Evan assured. "We'll find Lady Aine. We'll get her back."

"Speaking of whom," interrupted the bird who had taken a perch nearby. "I've seen her."

"What?" cried Evan, "You've seen Aine? Where?"

"Calm yourself, Foolish Boy! She's with those priests—the ones I didn't like."

Evan was too relieved to be annoyed with his Watcher, who in any event, was right. The obnoxious bird had warned him about Phillipus Mauritius, the imposter priest and Evan had refused to listen. "She's safe?" he begged, "Unharmed?"

Julian clucked and ruffled his feathers. "She's alive. They're headed toward the mountains and they have horses."

"Great heavens!"

"What does he say?" asked Martin.

"He's seen Lady Aine," Evan replied, "She's safe, but they have horses."

How would they manage to catch them now? The rescuers couldn't begin pursuit until nightfall, and by that time Aine might be anywhere. Still, it was a blessing to know she was alive.

The wounded were taken into the church to be tended by the King's surgeon, Torgal Umliath. The dead were stripped of armor and weapons and piled in a grisly pyramid to await burial. Both sides prepared for the next attack.

"You were wrong about the gate," chided Morleigh Dunroon as he caught sight of Anwend Halfdane.

"Don't be impatient. They'll settle on the gate soon enough. Besides, I said they'd go for the gate unless they were complete fools." He shrugged.

Morleigh grinned. "Perhaps we'll live long enough to see if you're right."

Anwend returned to his building program.

———————

The sun went down in a brilliant blaze of yellows and reds and a mixture of hues that defied description, but few people in Durham had the time to appreciate the sunset. It was doubtful that anyone was watching but Martin, who saw the light fade and wept from sadness that he might never see another sunrise.

Now that it was dark the four stout souls met in final preparation for their mission. The more they discussed their plans, the more panic clawed at Martin, sapping the strength he would need in the hours ahead.

It would have been simple to enter the river at the fortress dock, but lookouts had already seen small boats patrolling the river just beyond missile range of the walls. Accordingly they found another way. Rising from the confluence of the two rivers, a small cylindrical shaft of rough stone served as a conduit for all the waste and refuse from the palace. Though an awful place, it would provide access to the river beyond the sight of prying eyes.

Martin retied Lady Aine's favor about Evan's arm. The beautiful lace and embroidery were soiled and stained with dried blood making the cloth stiff and uncooperative.

"It's a shame this is ruined," said Martin as he finished the knot.

"We'll ask the lady to stitch us another," offered Evan.

Martin couldn't meet Evan's gaze.

"Look ye, Martin," said Evan, taking the boy by his trembling shoulders, "there's no need for you accompany me."

Martin's trepidation vanished before the greater spectre of being left behind. "No need? You need all the help you can get! I may not be much good, but I've pledged my life to you and your Lady. My life! Surely that's worth something. You mustn't go without me!"

"Indeed? And if I command it?"

"I wish you would not!"

"Such danger and hardship is beyond your experience. Why go?"

"Because Lady Aine is out there," Martin replied, and tears sprang to his eyes. "Because I can't stay here while my master risks his life. And if you try to make me stay, I'll disobey!"

Evan suppressed a smile as he considered his young servant. In other circumstances Martin's defiance might have landed him in irons, but at the moment, loyalty was of more value than decorum. "As you wish," Evan rejoined, throwing his arm about the boy, "but later I must punish you for your shocking behavior."

It was time to go. "God be with you," invoked Osric as he took their hands in turn. He embraced Evan. "When you've rescued her, find someplace safe until this unpleasantness is over."

"Don't be absurd," Evan insisted, "I'll be back before you can turn around." He returned his brother's smile, but it was impossible to dismiss the likelihood that they would never meet again.

"It's in God's Hands," Osric declared and the simple truth of the statement was a comfort amidst the surrounding fear and uncertainty.

The Four Stout Souls were escorted through the palace and down a narrow, uneven stair that wound its way into the depths of the Sceir Naid. As they descended, a terrible odor began to overwhelm their senses so that by the time they arrived at the bottom it was difficult to even breathe. Beyond a locked iron door, in a small room of roughly joined stone, the stench became palpable, sending even the redoubtable Padraigh staggering and retching. Rats squealed and scattered.

In the center of the uneven floor a sluggish stream of waste ran from an open gutter into a dark opening. Secured to an iron ring, a heavy rope hung down into the darkness, and one by one the four companions made the long descent into a

19

pool of unspeakable filth at the bottom of the shaft. From there it was a short, if unpleasant swim through an adjoining passage that led at last to the clear, cold water of the River Cuinn.

"Stay together," whispered Padraigh.

The night sky shone with the light from millions of stars that reflected from the dark water in dancing crystal glims. Though the moon had yet to rise, the shadowed outline of the town stood out as the current pulled them south. Fires illuminated both shorelines, and small boats slid through the water at either hand, but the companions slipped past undetected. Still, they had yet to deal with the Dragon Man's Ferry.

The only reliable way to cross the Cuinn near Durham was the Dragon Man's Ferry, so named for the aged operator who once claimed to have spotted a Water Dragon. A sizeable reward had been posted for the capture of the beast, and Evan remembered setting traps and fishing for the monster when he was a boy. But if there had ever been such a creature, no one ever managed to catch it.

Ahead of them, moored in the center of the channel, the barge stood silent sentinel. Torchlight glinted on spear points. Archers lined the rails. These men were fishing too, but not for the Water Dragon. The Four Stout Souls submerged.

Evan dove toward the murky bottom as the current pulled him rapidly south. He passed beneath the dim radiance of the ferry, stayed under as long as he could, and then came noiselessly up into the sweet night air.

That was simple enough, he thought. He saw Brian and Padraigh nearby, but not Martin. He was not to be found. "I should have made you stay behind," Evan whispered.

The watch fires along the shore receded and disappeared as they drifted with the current, and soon they began the long, arduous swim to the eastern shore. If they strayed any farther south they would have to deal with the treacherous Ciorram Eas. Evan left a prayer on the water in the hope that it might somehow find Martin.

———————

Martin dove beneath the surface with everyone else and let the river pull him rapidly along. In spite of the cold he decided that swimming wasn't so bad after all. The current was doing most of the work and soon they would all be on the far shore. The One True God did know how to swim!

Then he ran into something.

At first it was just a soft resistance as though he were walking through a curtain of gauze, but the impediment quickly became a clinging barrier that wrapped around him and held him fast. When he pushed, it offered no resistance. He tried to move back, but found himself entangled. He pulled for the surface and it draped over his head.

In wild terror Martin fought against the Water Dragon that had seized him. He kicked and punched and struggled with all his might and at last he burst to the surface.

Martin gulped for air, but the Dragon pulled him back into the cold, dark depths. Only it wasn't a Dragon. Just before he went under he glimpsed weed-encrusted ropes and realized he was tangled in the remains of an old fishing net.

His head pounded for air by the time he cut himself free and with the last of his strength he struggled to the surface. For a time he floated with the current, focused only on breathing.

Martin had just decided to swim for the shore when he heard the sound. At first he thought it many horses galloping in the distance, but instead of diminishing, the sound increased. As the gallop became a growl he realized he was headed for the falls.

With a cry of alarm he began swimming. He had never seen the falls, couldn't even remember what they were called, but he knew they were named after some obscure Glenmaran word meaning death, despair and destruction.

The angry river roared like some horrible beast as it hurled him around a sharp bend. He whipped past huge rocks, whirled around or glanced from their polished surfaces only to be slammed against others.

He swallowed water, struggled for air and was pulled under. The current bounced him off rocks and submerged trees and dragged him across the stones and gravel at the bottom before throwing him into the air long enough to draw a gasping breath.

Martin grabbed for an overhanging branch, but the water sucked him back to the bottom before he could reach it. He had seen terriers shake rats in their powerful jaws and now he knew how the rats felt. The last sound those hapless rodents heard was the horrible growl of the dog and the last he would ever hear was the rush and roar and scream of this angry river.

In a numbing burst of sound, amid torrents of water so severe that they bruised flesh, Martin hurtled over the Ciorram Eas and slammed into the river a hundred feet below. The impact drove the remaining air from his lungs while the current clawed at him, twisted him around, pulled him down once more and then deposited him into a quiet pool near the shore.

He couldn't believe he was alive, nor was he entirely certain he was. Bruised, cut, battered and disoriented, he gasped like a fish out of water—a fish that was very glad to be out of water.

The boy staggered up the bank. Well, the One True God could swim, but Martin didn't want to swim with Him anymore. He collapsed and slept.

Three Stout Souls shivered in the brush beside the river and watched a patrol of horsemen go by.

"We could use those horses," whispered Brian when they had passed. "If we surprised them . . ."

"Forget the horses," grumbled Padraigh. "The last thing we need is a fight. Sneak through. We've time. The Sceir Naid will hold for a while."

"We don't have time," argued Brian. "Without horses we'll never catch Claranides."

Padraigh's eyes narrowed. "That changes nothing. Whether you rescue the girl or not we've got to summon aid for the king. If you do something to bring Fitzwarren's lackeys down on us I'll kill you."

Brian's face turned dead with anger though he knew Padraigh was right. If to rescue Aine they failed to save the king, they had made a terrible bargain. "Understand?" hissed Padraigh.

Brian nodded. "You'll never kill me, Padraigh Rinn, but I understand."

The sudden arrival of Julian ended the argument.

"Where have you been?" demanded Evan.

"Spying," replied the bird.

"You might have been useful earlier. We lost Martin in the river."

"The Clumsy Boy? I regret to hear it."

"Have you learned anything?"

"The road to Faltigern is closely guarded. The whole countryside is full of armed men."

"And Aine?" asked Evan.

Julian shook his head. "Nothing more."

A blood moon hung in the eastern sky like a monstrous red eye, reflecting the slaughter of war engulfing Glenmara. In Durham the carnage of the first attack yet littered the edges of the Sceir Naid and wounded men on both sides still struggled for life. It was an awful, if familiar business, and one that showed no sign of soon ending.

Anwend Halfdane had just completed the final inspection of his building program when the alarm sounded and the forces of the rebellious dukes charged straight for the gate, carrying the trunk of a recently felled tree.

"You were right Varangian," Morleigh Dunroon cried from the wall. "Here they come for your gate!"

Anwend mustered his men. How he wished his own forty Varangian stalwarts were standing beside him! With those wild hearts he'd hold this pitiful gate, but they were quartered in the lower town and there had been no word of them.

Arrows took a heavy toll of the attackers, but the remainder continued up the stone ramp and across the bridge. At the ram's first blow dust sprang from the wood, mortar crumbled and stones dislodged from the walls. It was worse than Anwend had expected. The second impact tore one of the huge iron hinges from its mountings. Again and again the hollow echoes of the ram sounded over the town and with each blow the gates bulged and the stone cracked. Then with an abrupt roar and a cloud of choking dust, the gateway arch collapsed.

Anwend cursed. He hadn't imagined this. The true frailty of the gate had eluded even his practiced eye. He was both shocked and amused that so little effort had been required to topple it into a pile of twisted rubble--shocked because the sudden destruction had been so complete and amused because the ram and the unfortunates that carried it were buried in the debris.

As the dust settled on the mound of broken timber and shattered stone, a stunned silence descended on both sides. Then with a great cry the rebel army charged for the breach.

From the wall, Morleigh Dunroon directed fire on the advancing enemy. He hurled insults at the opposing archers, defying them to strike him. Missiles whirled past, shattered on the battlements, glanced from his armor but did not find their mark. The Duke laughed and taunted and capered atop the battlements, and soon many of the opposing archers were aiming at him. But whether because of darkness, poor aim, or the protecting Hand of Almighty God, no one could hit him.

Confident of victory, the attackers burst through into the palace yard. But instead of the courtyard they found themselves in an open-ended box surrounded on three sides by new walls of unmortared stone, bristling with soldiers. As the enclosure filled, the defenders hurled everything at hand, stones, darts, spears, even buckets of boiling water, into the packed masses before them.

But Anwend's wall wasn't very tall, and soon the attackers were clambering over it using their shields, each other, or the bodies of the slain to reach the top. Brutal fighting ensued along the entire length of the defensive works.

Osric stood to the wall side by side with his Varangian ally, slashing and stabbing at whatever tried to come over the top. They fought until they struggled for breath and staggered from exhaustion, and still the foe came in a desperate press to force the breach. With a last violent effort they broke through.

For a moment the yard began to fill with enemy soldiers, fighting their way past the defenders and up the broad palace steps. They could taste victory, but in a moment the taste turned bitter in their mouths. The palace doors burst open and the last of the Household Guard charged down the stairway. With a crash that rivaled the sound of the gatehouse falling, they flung themselves into Fitzwarren's men.

It was just enough. One moment the fate of the kingdom hung in the balance before the palace portals and in the next the attack fell apart. The enemy fled back over the wall, across the breach and into the upper town. Too exhausted to pursue, the defenders didn't follow.

"I will knight you when I can lift my sword again," Osric declared to Anwend.

"And I will gladly kneel to receive the accolade," replied the Varangian, "once I can summon the strength to rise so high."

Osric struggled to his feet, unwilling to rest in the presence of his subjects. Some had fallen together and lay side by side in death. Here the beautiful young wife of Lord Dunroon bandaged the leg of a wounded man-at-arms, and there a grizzled stable-hand cradled the head of a dying knight and spoke peace to him as he breathed his last. Osric moved among them, touched and spoke to them. They took comfort in his presence.

Throughout the night the enemy continued to probe the defenses, but no major attacks materialized. Still, long before sunrise, sentries reported the sounds of digging beneath the chapel.

I told you they'd go for the tunnel," said Dunroon with a sly wink at Anwend, "Anyone could have seen it."

The Varangian smiled. "Its solid rock! Where can they hope to dig in our lifetime?"

"We could send someone to find out," suggested Duke Eiolowen.

"It would be a death sentence for whoever went," observed Osric. "Fitzwarren can fill that tunnel with men and we haven't the forces to dislodge them. But if they dig into one of the lower storerooms . . ."

"Fill it with water!" Morleigh offered, "Let the dogs swim!"

"Have we a pump? Pipe of some kind?"

"We might stitch together hides."

"It would take all summer to make enough pipe," said Anwend dismissively, "and the balance of the year to flood the passage. We haven't time for that. But there's another option."

"Well, don't keep us guessing," smirked Dunroon. "We haven't time for that either."

Anwend nodded. "The tunnel slopes down from the church to the town below. A little oil and fire will have done with anyone skulking about down there."

"A sound plan," Osric agreed.

Retrieved from the cellars, barrels of oil were poured into the tunnel and a torch thrown after. They waited.

Soon all sorts of things began to happen. People streamed out of the house with the copper roof. Some tore off armor and smoldering clothing while others burst from the house fully ablaze, screaming and shrieking. Thick black smoke rolled out of doors and windows, and flames darted bright orange tongues into the night sky.

"You were right about the house Varangian," said Dunroon, his face strangely shadowed by the fire.

"Who owns that house?" Anwend asked of no one in particular.

"I don't know," answered Osric.

"A merchant, my lord. Baldwin Oakshotte, I believe," said someone.

At that moment, trapped by the flames in his beautiful copper roofed house, Baldwin Oakshotte huddled with his family in an upper room. He cursed his fate, cursed his ruined life, cursed Moloch and the One True God. This was all Claranides' fault. He looked at his wife, his son and tiny daughter and howled out in terror and despair. The sins of the father had come home to his family.

The fire went on to consume several other structures before it burned itself out toward morning. In the wake of the flames Baldwin Oakshotte's beautiful home was now a mound of broken stone, charred timbers and twisted, blackened copper. They had sealed the tunnel.

CHAPTER II
GWENFEREW

G iomer Lorich gazed across the meadow to the cemetery where forty patches of newly turned earth reflected the afternoon sunlight--an ironic contrast to the darkness and decay beneath that soil. He squeezed the hilt of his sword until his knuckles were as white as the ivory. Names and faces paraded through his mind, memories of simple events associated with the simple soldiers he had buried.

Three long, grey fingers found wedged beneath a rock remained the only clue to who or what had butchered his men. He had sent the requisite dispatches to authorities and even included a finger with each, but as yet there was no response. It was hardly surprising. Why would anyone be interested in such fairy-tale speculation? But there was nothing make-believe about forty dead legionaries.

The sound of riotous celebration shook Giomer out of his depressing reverie. In the town below, colorful parades marched through crowded streets, past scores of makeshift booths and shops where merchants offered a wide array of food and drink. Children chased each other through the press, squealing with delight. Acrobats performed feats of agility and skill. On the first day of Spring Festival, nearly everyone had joined in the fun, but in the Legion fortress, no one was having a good time.

Legionaries stood their posts in full kit while the rest of the garrison remained restricted to quarters. The timber walls and simple wooden towers enclosing the barracks, stables and armories also enclosed a rising current of discontent.

Commander Lorich wasn't insensible to the needs of his soldiers. Denying them the pleasures of Spring Festival wasn't an arbitrary decision. Other commanders might have shared their reasons for such an unpopular order, but he didn't take common soldiers into his confidence. They didn't need to be tucked into bed. Let them growl and stomp. He'd keep them alive—ready for the goblins that prowled the shadows.

If there were any goblins. Three fingers didn't prove much. One of his Centurions believed they were goblin fingers, but that speculation hadn't been enough to elicit a reaction from Mayor Isador Oxblood or Ajax the Anxious.

A petty politician, the Mayor didn't want goblin talk to spoil the festival. Legionaries may have been killed, but that didn't prove the town was in danger. Ajax Obrighdhu, the commander of the town militia, should have been more sympathetic to military concerns, but he didn't want to order his men to active duty during the celebration. After a lengthy argument, Ajax agreed to station a handful of men at each gate in the town palisade.

Giomer turned back to the fields of tall grass that rolled gently down to the mirror-calm waters of distant Loch Cuinn. The cavalry had scouted the countryside but found nothing. Everything appeared quiet and safe, and for the sake of the citizens celebrating outside the walls, he hoped it was safe. There were children out there.

He ran the numbers through his head once more, as though he hoped to find something more if he kept counting. Nothing had changed; four Centuries of one hundred men each, forty three auxiliaries who made up the artisans and skilled men, blacksmiths, armorers, carpenters, horse trainers and cooks, plus fifty cavalry troopers and their attendant supernumeraries. With two Tribunes and five Centurions, his command numbered slightly more than five hundred men—less the forty, forever less the forty.

Despite the promises of Ajax the Anxious, no militiamen stood at the gates. Not that their presence would have given Giomer much comfort. He recalled, without pleasure, how Ajax had earned his nickname.

Two years earlier a large raiding-party of Goths had crossed frozen Loch Cuinn and laid waste to outlying farms. With the Legion in earnest pursuit of the culprits, Ajax and the Gwenferew Militia mounted their own offensive.

The bitter temperature and heavy snowfall soon diminished whatever martial ardor they had mustered, and convinced Ajax that it was folly to wage war in such weather. When horrified scouts reported a large force of Goths advancing upon them, he led a mad retreat back to Gwenferew.

They barred the gates, manned the walls, and prepared for a desperate battle until the enemy appeared. Cows! An entire hungry herd had followed the startled militia all the way from the mountains. Thus had Ajax earned the sobriquet Ajax the Anxious. In honor of this legacy, some enterprising legionary secretly replaced the Timber Wolf banner of the Gwenferew Militia with the Banner of the Blue Cow. At the moment, Giomer found no humor in the affair.

To be fair, at least one member of the militia was on duty. Braslav Tlapinski had taken up residence in the western gate tower. Braslav waved. Giomer nodded, but quickly turned away. What a buffoon!

Braslav was an institution in Gwenferew. An avid gambler, he still lost more than he won. He drank to excess and ate more than most would have thought wise, though he displayed his incredible girth as if it were a trophy won through great effort. He dressed in garments decorated with expensive lace and gold thread, his wardrobe rivaling the wealthiest gentlemen in town, but his manner was coarse, and he told appalling lies. Still, he was a likable fellow in a bothersome way. Once by sheer force of presence he had barked down a crowd of townspeople intent on hanging two unfortunate legionaries during a seasonal anti-legion frenzy. This endeared him to the garrison that now considered him a sort of father figure.

Even so, there wasn't much benefit having Braslav on the wall.

Back at his quarters, Giomer tarried in the guardroom where the honors and war trophies of the Gwenferew detachment were displayed. The first legionaries had come here more than eighty years earlier when marauding Goths burned the original settlement. From the fortified Legion camp the thriving city of Gwenferew had taken form.

Of course, that had been long before his time. Most of the battle honors attached to the Second Glenmaran Border Legion had been won during savage wars with the Pictish tribes in the east: the battles of Manon's Ford, Corinth Glen, and Guilfrey's Hill. These names spoke the glory of the Second, but none so glorious as the Battle of Fort Cailte where 2300 legionaries held their fortified camp against a force of more than 25,000 Picts. Giomer had been but a raw recruit when he waded through the blood and terror of that awful battle, but he remembered it well--the hunger, the fear, the stench from thousands of unburied corpses. And the screams! Sometimes he could still hear the desperate cries of those taken alive by the Picts.

In spite of its horrors, despite the many good legionaries that had given their lives to hold that insignificant bit of terrain, it had been the seminal event in the history of the Second—a defining moment in the long history of the Border Legion in Glenmara.

More than 400 years before, when the mighty Legions of Ascalon conquered most of the known world, even Glenmara had been subjugated. Eventually, units were recruited from the conquered tribes to assist in the defense of the frontiers and from these beginnings the Border Legion had grown. When the great Glenmaran warrior Olcan Aonagan overthrew the Ascalonian invaders, the structure of these independent units was retained.

Now there were two Legions in Glenmara; the First, deployed along the southern and western frontiers, and the Second, assigned to guard the north and east. When it came to a stand-up fight, the Border Legions always held their own, and that was a good thing, for unless Giomer was much mistaken, it would come to a stand-up fight very soon.

The sun dipped below the mountains, reflecting from the lake in the last bit of shadowed clarity before true darkness descended. In the town the celebration went on, beneath the light of lamps and torches. People staggered senseless through the streets.

Braslav watched. He was good at watching-- and waiting. He had made it a life work. Patience and a keen sense of knowing when something was afoot were his greatest allies. But at the moment, anyone could have recognized that something was afoot. While the people rutted about like drunken fools with the city gates flung open, the Legion stood to arms behind their fortress walls. So Braslav volunteered to man the gate tower near the Legion compound.

He spoke with the Legion guards, disguising his inquiries with rambling stories and pointless banter, but learned nothing. Eventually he gathered whatever free food and drink he could get from the merchants he knew--which wasn't much since he owed most of them money--and retired to the tower. He hated to miss the debauchery and excitement of Spring Festival, but alarms had been going off in his head for weeks. Strange visions haunted him, filling his mind with portents and warnings.

He still wasn't used to the visions. Since childhood, his confused, disjointed dreams had always held some vestige of the truth. Sorting the truth from the fantasy was the problem. For instance, when he was a boy he dreamt that his brother Ivan found a jar of gold coins while plowing a field. Later, a different man named Ivan found the treasure. Another time he dreamt of fire in his neighbor's barn, but three weeks later his own family's barn burned to the ground.

Sometimes a feeling of contentment would descend upon him, often indicating that something good was about to happen--maybe not specifically to him, but if he were watchful and inquisitive, more often than not he could profit from the good fortune of others. Just as often, a sense of dread would herald the approach of something unpleasant, requiring equal attention.

There was no doubt that Braslav had 'the vision,' though it was less than *perfect* vision.

In his forty-three years Braslav had been a farmer, a deck hand aboard an Illyrian merchantman, a soldier, a freebooter, sometimes bandit and a professional gambler. But his uncontrollable 'gift' always encouraged him to change professions before long. Being able to divine what was going to happen, however inaccurately, was often more liability than asset.

Today, if he had to define his profession it would have been 'advisor' or 'consultant.' He smiled at the notion. He didn't really advise or consult on anything but he managed to insinuate himself into other people's business often enough to be included in a wide variety of profitable ventures. It was such a venture that had kept him in Gwenferew when indications all around him were urging him to flee.

For several weeks an inescapable sense of darkness and fear had occupied his thoughts asleep and awake. The unfortunate deaths of those poor Legion lads had reinforced the dread, convincing Braslav that something awful was about to happen. Still, with his poor 'sight,' it might just as well happen in Durham.

Nonetheless he thought enough of the potential to spend the day in the otherwise abandoned tower, armed and in armor. It appeared he would be spending the night there too. He would have preferred his own bed to the cold, drafty battlements, but he wanted to remain close to the Legion if something happened. He hoped he wouldn't regret his decision to stay.

He sipped wine from a small flagon he had brought with him. He liked wine, drinking altogether more than he should. But not today. Never mind he had such a scant supply; tonight wasn't a good time to get drunk. He would have eaten something from his small supply of food, but the smell was becoming quite distracting.

The breeze blowing up from the lake carried an awful stench. Those stupid butchers must have been slaughtering animals out there again, leaving the remains to ferment in the sun. Braslav sniffed and frowned. The smell was getting worse.

It was difficult to distinguish the first cries of terror from the general noise of the merry making. But soon sounds of panic and death overpowered everything else.

Legion sentries called out warning. A sudden rush of people through the western gate was followed by total chaos. Things swarmed after the fleeing citizens; strange, shadowed shapes that danced from side to side in the dim light. Where they danced people went down and didn't get up.

"Will ya look! There's thousands of 'em! We're in fer it now!" howled one of the sentries.

"Shut yer mouth!" ordered an Optio, "Go fetch the officer. Now, d'ya hear! Boy, blow that trumpet of yours. Stand to yer posts ya quavering dogs!"

As alarms sounded, the Legion compound stirred with life. Legionaries spilled from their barracks pulling on helmets and wrestling equipment into place. Giomer vaulted up the ladder to the battlements with an agility that belied his age, arriving to find the bazaar outside in flames, the sward covered with bodies. The same terrible odor that had begun the night before was now nearly overpowering.

At the gate, frantic citizens tried to claw their way into the city over the bodies of their fellows. People were trampled, crushed, violently thrust aside as they fought to reach safety, but Giomer knew that unless the walls were manned, the city would offer no safety at all. As if in response to that realization, a dozen or more grey creatures swarmed onto the parapet.

The sentries hesitated until Giomer dispatched the first goblin to come near. Galvanized by their commander, the legionaries cleared the battlements in one violent rush. Giomer leaned down and examined the squat grey form of the dead goblin, the long, powerful arms and short, muscular legs. Hideous orange eyes stared sightlessly into the night sky while long, narrow fingers twitched in the last tremors of death. Giomer grunted. Goblin fingers. But there wasn't time to contemplate such things. He called to the legionaries gathered in the fortress yard.

"First Century to the walls! Second and Third muster at the gate! Fourth stand fast. Officers to me!"

Goblins clambered across the ditch at the base of the town wall. Still more emerged from the dark meadows beyond the town and poured through the gateway in pursuit of the fleeing townsfolk.

With his officers gathered about him, Giomer's eyes sparkled with grim excitement. It was a warrior's moment, the heady thrill that came with every battle, intensified by the fact that he had been right all along. But though he had kept his command intact, though he had correctly predicted what the enemy would do, the next few hours would be more crucial than any that had already passed.

In the past days he had played the scenario out in his mind again and again even though he had no idea how goblins fought or what they were likely to do in any situation. But the last few minutes had revealed much about the enemy. Beyond their superior numbers and the excellent quality of their arms and armor, the most disturbing thing was the hundreds of crude ladders the goblins had brought with them--ladders just long enough to rest at the bottom of the ditch and easily hook over the top of the palisade. They had known the height of the wall beforehand.

"They intended to take us celebrating," he said, "but we've put paid to that plan. Now we'll show them what we intend to do. Orri, take your cavalry and secure the gate. Ronan, take the second Century into the plaza and keep the goblins away from Orri. Dermott, stand fast for orders. Einar, you're in reserve. Now move!"

Fifty cavalry troopers thundered out into the plaza, and the sudden appearance of horses amongst the goblins was like mixing oil and water. Most had never seen a horse before and they didn't like what they saw now. The horses, though nervous at the unfamiliar sight and smell of goblins, charged into them rending flesh and trampling bodies beneath their iron-shod hooves. Atop the terrible creatures armored men lay into the goblin ranks with spear and sword, driving them back, while from the fortress wall came a supporting hail of arrows, darts and stones.

But the success of the cavalry was immediately threatened by several hundred goblins already in the town who formed ranks and advanced across the plaza. The second century quickly moved to engage them, and a fierce battle commenced.

More goblins pushed through the gate, threatening to overwhelm the small cavalry troop; they pulled riders from their saddles and cut them to pieces. Horses fell screaming, pierced by goblin steel. As the legionaries gave ground, Giomer committed the third century.

With the arrival of more humans, the goblin infantry scattered across the plaza, but another group quickly took their place. Goblins continued to pour through the open gateway.

Giomer summoned Centurion Einar, whose depleted century had already suffered from goblin steel. "Some of those goblins carry the weapons they took from your men," Giomer explained, "and one of them is missing fingers."

The Centurion's face twisted as he watched the swarm of grey below. "You've got to close that gate or none of us will see the sunrise," Giomer said. He looked into Einar's intelligent, experienced eyes, and knew he would need every bit of that intelligence and experience to live out the next few minutes.

"I'll come from over there," Einar declared, indicating a section of the west wall, and before Giomer could respond, Einar leapt from the wall walk and sprinted over to his waiting men.

———

Einar Thangmartsen told his men what they were going to do. There were no questions. Legionaries didn't question orders. They went where they were told, fought where they were told and died where they were told; unquestioning obedience was one of the qualities that made legionaries so fearsome in battle. Sixty-three men followed their Centurion through a small gate into the narrow maze of city streets.

Sounds of terror filled the night--screams, cries for mercy or help. Goblins looted homes and shops whose occupants lay in unnatural poses on the bloody cobblestones. Twice the legionaries were interrupted by bands of goblins that, taking them for fleeing citizens, rushed upon them. None survived long past realizing their mistake.

As the legionaries wound their way toward the western wall, avoiding combat except that thrust upon them, scores of desperate citizens attached themselves to Einar's little command. They demanded protection for their families and property, and since Einar couldn't help them, they followed behind weeping and cursing and calling the soldiers terrible names.

The entourage continued to grow, an inconvenience Einar hadn't anticipated. Yet many of the townsfolk, though frightened, disoriented and convinced that the end of the world was upon them, pried stones from the streets, tore the staves from barrels and gathered anything they might utilize as a weapon. If the Legion would fight, so would they. By the time they reached the western gate, Einar's command had more than doubled.

Without hesitation, Einar attacked the flank of the goblin column coming through the gate, and the last of Gwenferew's legionaries were committed to the fight. At a dead run, in a tight wedge of locked shields and bristling swords they scythed through the enemy as though a single massive blade had been swung out of the darkness by an unseen giant.

Goblin formations in the plaza gave ground to renewed pressure from the second and third centuries. But the battle wasn't yet won. Giomer stripped every third man from the battlements and led them into the fray. With Giomer's small force added to the line, the legionaries pushed the enemy back and cleared the gate. But there were still thousands of goblins milling about outside, and when the humans failed to pursue, the goblins began to rally.

Einar knew that if the gate remained open the Legion couldn't withstand the goblin counter-attack, but when he pushed against the massive wooden portal it refused to move. The mechanism was locked open, and to free it he would have to get inside the gate tower.

While Einar tried to force his way inside, Braslav huddled on the second floor. With goblins both above and below doing their best to get at him, he cursed the events that had brought him to such a disastrous end. His watery, bulging eyes cast about for an escape but found none. He mopped his sweat soaked face with a dirty sleeve. "Fie on these grey fellows!" he wailed and drew out his heavy sword.

He laughed hysterically as he slashed the poorly balanced cutlass through the air. It was the same weapon he had carried as a sailor, but he had rarely used it then, and not at all for some years. "Is this the end of Braslav?" he wept, and at that moment the trap door above him burst open.

With wild cries, goblins leapt into the room. Braslav flailed away with his cutlass, grunting, wheezing and occasionally letting out a horrible choking cry as he blundered about the room. Yet even in his mindless frenzy he managed to inflict some damage and one unfortunate goblin staggered back clutching at the stump of his arm. The strange, deadly dance continued until the goblins managed to open the trap door to the lower room, allowing more of their brethren to swarm up the ladder.

What happened next might have been comical had the results not been so deadly. Encouraged by the arrival of their companions, the goblins rushed Braslav who stumbled, tripped, and fell through the hatchway, carrying those ascending the ladder down with him. With a combined scream, the mass of pink and grey flesh impacted the hard earthen floor.

For a moment no one stirred, the goblins a motionless heap beneath the insensate human. Braslav showed the first signs of life, gasping for air and floundering about in the tangle of grey arms and legs. Once able to breathe, he marveled at his survival. Of the goblins that had cushioned his fall, most didn't move at all and those that did whimpered and hissed in pain. Yet there was one goblin still capable of action, and he came after Braslav with murder in his eyes.

Struggling to regain his feet and find his sword, Braslav's hand closed around a large wooden lever set into the wall. He heaved himself up with a great cry but fell as the lever shifted, and though falling saved him from the sword that sliced the air just above his head, there was no way to protect against the next blow.

Poised to part Braslav's head from his shoulders, the goblin flinched from the sudden frightful explosion of sound that filled the chamber. A massive mechanism of chains, counterweights, and gears clanked, squealed, and rumbled into life. Yet the respite provided by the accidental activation of the gate apparatus wouldn't have been sufficient to save Braslav had not the tower door burst open and the room filled with legionaries. The hapless goblin was dead before he could react.

Einar pulled a wide-eyed Braslav to his feet. "We came to shut the gate," said the Centurion, "but I see you had matters well in hand." As unbelievable as it seemed, the evidence was plain; Braslav had closed the gate.

One of the legionaries handed Braslav his cutlass. "Busy work, ain't it, father?"

"Busy indeed, but the type of work I'm quite familiar with."

"You know 'bout goblins, father?"

"Men or goblins, it's all the same to me. They flee or fall before Braslav's steel!"

With the battle still raging, Einar couldn't long contemplate the paradox of Braslav. He gathered his men, assigned several to guard the gate tower and led the remainder back to the plaza.

"Will you come with us, Braslav?" called Einar from the doorway. "You'd be useful on the wall."

Braslav shook his head. "Certainly not! I paid for this tower with my own blood!" he declared, displaying an abrasion on his massive forearm. "Go to your battle and I'll keep guard here!"

Einar grinned and went back outside.

With the gate secure, Giomer dispatched the goblins that remained in the plaza. Yet beyond the palisade, the grey tide gathered. The battle had only begun.

No one dared approach Klabaga, the singular Red Goblin in Ugrik's army. His appearance was intimidating enough; tall and manlike in proportion, his copper-red flesh rippled with hard muscle. But tonight his yellow eyes were filled with rage, for while the rest of the eight thousand strong goblin army assaulted the man-town, Klabaga had been left to guard the roadway.

He listened as the distant sounds of panic became the echoes of battle; echoes that belied the notion of token resistance. His mood continued to deteriorate until just before dawn when he could no longer stand the inaction.

"Orglyx," he snapped, "take command till I comes back!"

Klabaga followed the roadway through the sea of tall grasses at either hand. The heavy odor of smoke hung in the air, and the uneven glow against the dark horizon grew in intensity. Then, beyond the crest of a low hill, Gwenferew came abruptly into sight.

Backlit by the burning town, the entire western wall swarmed with combat. Goblins scrambled up ladders only to be met by spear and sword and thrown violently down into the packed masses below. There were so many goblins concentrated into such a small area that they stumbled into one another and milled about as though they were blind. Nearby, Ugrik directed the assault.

"Madness," mumbled the Red Goblin. He hurried back to his command. He hadn't come all this way to guard a road, and he didn't intend to join the chaos Ugrik had created. Instead he led his soldiers toward the river.

Dawn approached. Shadows grew less comforting, gradually giving way to an even less appealing half-light. Though much of the army was occupied in storming the west wall, Klabaga discovered the plain south of the city was full of goblins pillaging the tents, booths and wagons abandoned by their human owners. As he proceeded, he incorporated these stragglers into his column.

The south gate of the man-town was barred, but the walls and towers appeared unmanned. Arriving at the river, the Red Goblin found the shore crowded with humans, pushing and shoving their way onto the docks and the great wooden bridge.

At the arrival of the goblins, cries of panic and dismay erupted from the fleeing humans. Chaos reigned. With screams of despair, people leapt into the river to drown in the swift current. Others tried to force passage on already overcrowded boats or joined the hopeless snarl of humanity crossing the bridge. Still more fled back into the city to seek refuge within its walls. Some goblins went wild at the sight and fell upon the humans wholesale, slashing and slaying. They carried away women and ransacked the packages, boxes and bales left behind. But most obeyed orders and remained in formation as they moved toward the eastern gate. Finding it thrown open, the goblin formation rushed into the town.

"On the right into line!" Klabaga barked, and with easy precision his soldiers took up battle formation in four ranks. "Orglyx, secure that gate!

I wants goblins in that tower! Move ya dim-witted lot!" Within moments the eastern city wall was firmly in goblin hands. The rest waited for orders, casting curious glances at the strange architecture, sniffing the unfamiliar smells that filled the sun-warmed morning air.

A harsh staccato rhythm echoed from the interior of the town. Klabaga tried to identify it, for it grew louder by the moment, and soon it was accompanied by the shouts and screams of goblins. A rush of fear washed over the Red Goblin as the unseen menace approached, but his orders were clear, calm, and instantly obeyed. "Guard against cavalry! Move!" The goblin formation became a hollow square, bristling with spears like a vast, grey porcupine. No sooner had this change taken place than a band of terrified goblins burst into the plaza pursued by human-men on horses.

"Hold formation! Tighten the line! I'll kill the first goblin what flinches!"

The horsemen were already riding down their hapless prey, slashing them with swords, impaling them on lances. The few that reached Klabaga's formation tried to force their way through to safety, but the line refused to open. Instead it braced for the impact.

The horses charged down upon the barrier of steel and when it held fast, the steeds made an effort to slow their headlong pace. In that hesitant moment a hail of spears brought death and confusion. Men and mounts went down in a tangle of screams and flailing limbs. Before the humans could refocus their efforts, the hollow square split, wheeled around and enveloped the humans like a wave, cutting off any possibility of retreat. Only a handful managed to win free. The rest were cut down in the ensuing melee.

When the butchery was over, Klabaga re-formed his ranks and gestured at the surrounding carnage. "D'ya see?" he snarled. "They sent human men on horses and we destroyed 'em. They can send trolls or ogres or dragons and we'll give 'em the same. Follow me and one day we'll rule the world of men!"

The Grey Goblins slammed swords against shields and screamed out their battle cry of "Ulu! Ulu! Ulu!" again and again. After this victory, their loyalty to the Red Goblin was assured.

Klabaga left a detachment to hold the gate and led the rest of his command into the strange interior of the Man City. The closely packed buildings offered comforting shadows that lingered in defiance of the risen sun. Some of the strange dwellings were on fire and charred human bodies lay strewn about the streets, mute evidence that goblins had already been there. But it was also apparent that at the moment, Klabaga commanded the only organized goblin force within the walls.

They came to the Town Square.

———

Optio Tyrus was more frustrated and anxious than he had ever been. He was frustrated because no one would listen to him and he was anxious because the sounds of battle at the west wall reached all the way to the Town Square. He shifted his grip on the short sword in his hand.

But though he wanted to come to grips with the goblins, he was just as anxious to grip Isador Oxblood by the throat. The Mayor had locked himself in the town hall and refused to come out. Standing atop his third floor balcony wrapped in a white blanket, Isador resembled an immense egret.

"Won't you listen to reason?" implored Tyrus.

"Listen to reason?" the Egret screeched, "What reason is there to come out of a fortified building?"

Tyrus snarled. "Then send Ajax. We must secure the gates."

"Secure the gates? A bit late for that isn't it? And what's the Legion doing anyway?"

A panicked flood of humanity continued to crowd into the plaza, bumping and jostling each other as they attempted to gain entry to the Town Hall. No one was listening to a simple Optio.

"Let me speak to Ajax," demanded Tyrus, stung by the mayor's dismissal and the muffled laughter of the legionary squad behind him.

The mayor shrugged and shook his head.

"I must speak to Ajax!" insisted Tyrus.

"That's Commander Ajax to you," sounded an imperious voice. Ajax stepped out onto the balcony.

From his finely wrought maille to the jewel-encrusted sword at his side, Ajax Obrigdhu looked every inch the warrior. Even his bearing indicated calm reaction to the surrounding chaos, but Tyrus knew that was only because the fellow was standing twenty feet above the street.

"*Commander*," said Tyrus, careful to keep the sarcasm out of his voice, "We need your troops on the wall."

"Don't tell me my business!" responded Ajax. "If Giomer wants something, let him ask."

"He's busy at the moment. He sent me to muster the militia."

Ajax spat off the balcony. "I command the militia, not Giomer. We are mustering here to protect the seat of government. We will not go piecemeal to the walls." With that announcement, both he and the Mayor withdrew.

Tyrus cursed, though he knew that even mustered, the militia would be of little use with Ajax in charge. Still, orders were orders. If reason wouldn't work perhaps intimidation would. He faced his men. "Squad, 'shun!" he bellowed and the eight-man detachment snapped to attention. "I'm going to see if I can talk some sense into those empty heads in there. You lot force us a way into that building. Try not to kill anyone, but get us inside. Forward, March!"

The main entrance to the town hall was crowded with people, packages, and piles of belongings, but the Legion squad pushed its way through in a tight wedge. Optio Tyrus staged his men between two great stairways.

"Stand fast," he ordered. "Angus, you're in charge until I get back. Donagh with me."

Tyrus shoved Donagh up the stairs. Though not a large man, Donagh's strength was legendary among the legionaries in Gwenferew. He could pull a fully laden oxcart unaided and once, at the urging of his mates, he split a legionary shield from rim to boss with a single sword blow, though the cost of the shield had been deducted from his pay. Donagh was easily led in the wrong direction, but with him in the lead they got up the stairs.

At the top of the landing an open doorway marked the entrance to the council hall. The long, narrow room was already full of bewildered people and it was only with great difficulty that the two legionaries managed to squeeze through the press to the heavy door at the far end. Beyond this locked portal, stairs mounted to the mayor's personal rooms.

The Optio pounded at the door but got no response. Donagh pounded too, with such power and violence that dust sprang from the timbers, but still there was no answer.

"Hiding?" mused Tyrus and pulled Donagh onto an adjacent balcony. Above them the windows of Isador Oxblood's residence beckoned.

"Lift me up," said Tyrus, and as effortless as the thought Donagh hoisted the Optio onto his broad shoulders and heaved him up onto the balcony. With a leap and a hand from the Optio, Donagh followed, but here also the door was barred.

"Open it," Tyrus commanded.

The door swung back in splinters from the force of Donagh's kick.

A wild scramble erupted inside the room. People fell over furniture in surprise, certain the goblins were upon them. Some drew steel and prepared to defend their families and kin.

"The Legion has come!" someone cried out. "Hurrah for the Legion!"

Anxious merchants and members of the Town Council surrounded Tyrus.

"What shall we do?"

"Where is Giomer?"

"You can't come in here!" shrieked Isador, trying to bolster his courage with the volume of his voice. "These are my private chambers. I'll see you pay for that door!"

The Optio spat on the floor. "There won't be a building left to hang a door on if we don't muster the militia," he snarled, and Isador's features blanched as though cold water had been thrown in his face, "I want every man that can hold a weapon mustered in the square. Right now, or I'll put you all in chains!"

Ajax laid hand to sword hilt. "You go too far, Optio," he protested.

"Draw steel on me and your worries are over *commander*," Tyrus said with such simple conviction that Ajax let his hand fall away from the weapon, "Either command your men or I'll take command from you. Choose."

Ajax hesitated as he studied the menace in the Optio's eyes. Though the prospect of facing goblins was daunting, his chief worry was living out the next few minutes. He nodded. "Muster in the square!" he roared with sudden conviction.

The sight of armed men forming up on the cobblestones evoked a calming effect. A certain order began to overcome the panic as the militia stood to arms and before long nearly two hundred men patiently awaited orders.

Yet just when it seemed that discipline might overcome chaos, goblins appeared at the far side of the square. The crowd cried out in dismay. Ajax swore a blasphemous oath and took a step toward the town hall. Before Tyrus could regain control, the militia scattered.

Klabaga, however, maintained complete control. The Grey Goblins rushed forward and by the time they were done, the militia was either trapped in the hall or lay dead on the street.

In the Town Hall, Tyrus immediately set about organizing a defense, but the goblins didn't press their attack. From the balcony the Optio saw them waiting between the buildings bordering the square. "What are they at?" he wondered out loud.

He didn't wonder long. Tyrus had barely seen that all the doors and windows were secured when Donagh called him back to the balcony. "There's more of 'em," the legionary reported.

Tyrus noted additional enemy formations marching into the square. Rank upon rank flooded across the paving stones in a coiling grey tide. The morning sun glinted from their weapons and armor as they turned onto the main boulevard that led to the western gate and the Legion fortress. They howled and yammered as they passed, making strange gestures and mouthing indecipherable words that couldn't have been remotely polite or pleasant, but they didn't attack the town hall. They were going for the Legion fortress. If it fell, Tyrus and everyone in the town hall would be doomed.

The goblin attack was no longer a haphazard affair. Now it was organized and focused with deadly intensity. Tyrus couldn't know it, but the change was all Klabaga's doing. It was he who had opened the southern gate and summoned Greebo. It was he who had started the goblin columns marching toward the Legion camp, leaving Ugrik howling impotently at the fastness of the Western Wall. It was Klabaga who had suddenly changed the entire complexion of the battle for Gwenferew.

———

The first indication that conditions had worsened was the appearance of hundreds of panicked people in the western plaza. A large goblin force followed close on their heels.

Giomer cursed. The plaza was now so crowded with frantic citizenry that it was impossible to maneuver troops to meet the new threat. He ordered the fortress gates opened and the townsfolk poured inside where they were unceremoniously shoved into empty barracks and other Legion buildings. Soon legionaries were in combat with the first goblin column. The commander issued orders, bugles blew and the Legion began an organized retreat.

Einar hurried back to the gate tower. "Destroy that thing," he said gesturing to the gate mechanism, "and fall back to the fortress."

While the legionaries pried and twisted at the gears and chains, Braslav approached Einar. "What's happening?" he asked, eyes wide with fear.

"The town is lost," said Einar. He pointed to the east where Legion companies struggled to hold back the grey hordes. Others fell back from their positions on the walls, retreating in disciplined order toward the fortress. Goblins swarmed over the unprotected barrier.

Braslav gasped and staggered. For the second time that day he faced his startling lack of bravery and his terrible fear of death. Einar steadied him.

"Take heart!" he said with a smile and a wink, "They'll not find the fortress such an easy nut to crack. Legion steel will stop them yet."

Einar's calm demeanor in the midst of the swirling, screaming chaos was heartening, but Einar was a Centurion--he was supposed to be calm when everything was falling apart. If the officers showed fear, even the bravest legionaries would break. As it was, with the retreat hard pressed, if just one Optio lost control of his men, they might lose the entire battle.

The legionaries came tumbling out of the gate tower. "We've jammed the gate right proper sir," one reported with a grin.

Einar slapped him on the shoulder. "Good. Now go join the others." They hurried off.

"What about me?" quailed Braslav.

"Come, father," Einar encouraged, "once you're safe inside . . ." He was interrupted by the appearance of an errant goblin, but a quick parry and a well-aimed thrust sent the creature crashing to the ground. When the Centurion turned back, Braslav was already disappearing through the fortress gate.

———————

When the screaming began, Giomer Lorich retreated to his quarters and tried to stop his ears with the heels of his hands. It was happening all over again. The siege. The screams. This time it was goblins instead of Picts, and Giomer was the commander instead of a common legionary, but none of that mattered. The nightmare of Fort Cailte was upon him once again.

The Legion compound was crammed with so many frightened civilians that there was hardly any place to put them. They filled the barracks, kitchens and stables and spilled out to clog the streets and common areas in a confused sea of humanity. Many had brought household possessions, livestock and other domestic animals with them, further complicating the effective defense of the fort.

For their part, the goblins made no move to attack the Legion fortress. They withdrew beyond the range of spears and arrows and began the systematic looting of the town. What they didn't want they smashed, littering the street with debris. Prisoners were chained together and herded away with spear-points to an unimaginable fate. But as terrible as it was for the legionaries on the walls to watch the captives being driven away, to hear their pleas for help and be unable to do anything, far worse were the screams of those the goblins had selected for torture.

On the edge of the plaza, within full view of the Legion fortress, with blades and fire and heated iron, the goblins tortured dozens of people. Their screams and shrieks fed the helpless rage of the legionaries and kept Giomer locked in his rooms.

The goblins taunted and gestured, forcing Legion Officers to keep their men in place with threats and the flats of their swords. Less disciplined men would have rushed out to their doom, but as it was, standing to their posts, many battle hardened veterans wept.

Legion archers searched for targets, but the squat, grey creatures were careful to stay out of range. One particularly bold goblin, however, danced and cavorted right at the edge of where Legion arrows might reach. His antics attracted a lot of arrows.

An Optio shoved his way onto the battlements to snatch the short, re-curved bow from the hands of a startled archer. "You're wasting arrows!" he snarled. "Them grey fellows got no bows. Use up yer arrows and they'll send ya none in return. Next man that wastes an arrow will answer ta me!"

"But Optio," protested the hapless bowman, "look at that pig out there. Oh for a stouter bow!"

The Optio looked out over the plaza and scowled. "Legion equipment ain't good enough fer ya?" He seized an arrow from the legionary's quiver, drew the shaft back to his cheek and let fly. "It ain't the bow," he said, tossing it back to its owner.

The confused legionary turned to the prancing goblin just in time to see the creature stagger and fall, an arrow sunk to the fletching in his chest. A wild roar went up from the men on the wall and the Optio was hailed an instant hero. After that, the goblins stayed farther away, but the torture and screaming continued.

In the absence of their commander, Tribunes Ronan and Arden worked to restore order in the chaotic camp. Women and children were gently ushered out of the way while able-bodied men and boys were organized into manageable units, armed and marched away.

The goblins continued their depredations. Before morning waned into afternoon, they had consolidated their positions in the town and Ugrik turned his attentions to the Legion fortress and the town hall. But as Klabaga saw to the disposition of his soldiers, his mind could focus on but one thing: Evan MacKeth.

While everyone else in the Legion compound tried to stop their ears against the screams of those being tortured by the goblins, Braslav Tlapinski tried to stop his mind.

It was happening again. The terrible visions--glimpses of an uncertain future etched with images of destruction and death. He saw an endless plain filled with corpses, death birds tearing at sightless eyes, and through the carnage stalked a formless horror of darkness, despair and over-whelming hatred. He was all too familiar with this spirit and what it brought in its wake. The small village in Illyria struck by the plague within a week of his first such vision. The huge wave that had totally destroyed the seacoast town of Tynne. The vision of this spirit always portended doom, and now it had finally run him to ground. He re-called what his father had told him.

"You can't run from a gift like yours. Learn to use it my boy."

The hideous symphony in his head, a gift? Of what use were the disturbing images of fire, tor-ture, and blood if he couldn't escape them? But amidst the cacophony of fear and destruction, a voice he had never heard before began whispering words he couldn't decipher. Braslav wept and tried to hide.

———————

By the time the goblins turned their attention to the Town Hall, Optio Tyrus had completed the final inspection of the little force at his command. He had opened the town arsenal and distributed weapons to every man, woman, and child. He saw to their dispositions, assigned a legionary to each group and gave simple instructions. "Don't let them in. Whatever else happens, don't let them inside!" And when the attack came, they obeyed.

The goblins were met with such determined resistance that they drew back in dismay. Confronted with a bristling hedge of spears from the windows and a deadly rain of missiles from the balconies, the attackers retreated in disarray.

Before the defenders had time to congratulate themselves, the goblins came at the main entrance with heavy timbers to batter in the doors. But the doors were strong, and soon grey bodies blocked the portals. The goblins turned back to the windows only to be brutally repulsed again.

During a lull in the fighting Tyrus gathered those too old or too young to fight and set them to distributing food and water. They were holding their own, but without help they couldn't hold for long. The goblins would eventually route them out, burn the place down over their heads and dance among their bones, but before that happened Tyrus would make them pay for their victory.

CHAPTER III
PURSUIT

S itting in a corner of the crude hut, Aine accepted the bowl of thin broth, though she knew that the peasant woman who offered it could ill afford to feed unexpected visitors. Still, after a day and night on horseback, she welcomed the food, wherever it came from, and the tiny house, though filthy, seemed a regal accommodation. She finished the last of the broth and leaned back with a sigh.

"Good?" asked Eowulf.

Her eyes blazed contempt.

Eowulf snatched the empty bowl and stalked over to the fire, where he filled it again. He didn't understand Aine at all, but then, there had never been much understanding between Eowulf Fitzwarren and women.

He could scarcely countenance such complicated things as relationships. They were frustrating, unpredictable, incomprehensible. He might have kidnapped Aine, but apart from beating her unconscious he hadn't been cruel. Her virtue was still intact--so far. He wanted her to come to him willingly, and why shouldn't she? She could do worse than the son of a Duke! Her father was only a Baron. Still, revisiting such old thoughts brought uneasy memories of other girls in other situations—unfortunate incidents of un-reciprocal affection. They had been such pretty girls . . . He shuddered and drank his soup in a single swallow.

Eowulf tossed the bowl back to the peasant woman and strode to the doorway. The moon cast a pastel of brightness across the shadowed landscape making the darkness seem less severe. But even with the extra light, it was difficult to be certain of what he was looking at. He glanced over his shoulder where Claranides and his fellow clerics had arrayed themselves against one wall, and was struck with the uneasy realization that no manner of light could adequately reveal the sinister secrets hidden behind those dark eyes.

The High Priest's countenance betrayed nothing, but his mind was seething with schemes. Escape to the Hinnom Valley wasn't the only thing to consider. The thoughts that now crowded his mind had begun in the church atop the Sceir Naid as his plans disintegrated before his eyes. When his desperate call for an avenger had gone unanswered, for a time he had doubted his own faith. He had even entertained the heretical thought that Iosa Christus might be more powerful than Moloch. Yet in the end he had come to the realization that his efforts had failed for one simple reason: the God wanted blood.

He found it amusing that he had overlooked that basic requirement. You couldn't expect an answer to prayer without ritual blood sacrifice--no blood, no avenger. But though they had failed in the church, there would be ample time for sacrifice once they reached the Temple.

Claranides studied Aine Ceallaigh. Pretty, young and noble-born. They would have their avenger yet.

By dawn, the Three Stout Souls were well clear of the river, but lacking horses their progress remained dismally slow. With a steady, rhythmic pace they traversed the brush, streams and uneven ground of the countryside, avoiding the roads that might have hastened their journey.

Even in the midst of despair Evan had time to wonder at the power and mercy of God. As Evan followed Padraigh at a brisk trot across an overgrown meadow and up a hillside, he felt as though he had never been ill. Though he would gladly have traded his health to have Aine back safe and sound, he knew God didn't work that way. His mind wandered to happier moments.

"If the One True God is merciful, why does He allow so many terrible things to happen? Where's the mercy in that?"

Julian Antony Vorenius shook his head and smiled. "He doesn't have anything to do with that. Things happen, sometimes good, sometimes bad. But if you walk with Iosa, even bad things can work for good."

The boy scratched his head. "What sense does that make? How can bad be good? Can't the One True God just stop bad things from happening?"

"He can do as He likes," said Julian with a shrug, "He has intervened in our wicked ways before, but don't blame Him for the evils of the world"

"Then is it the Shadow Lord? Dark Things?"

"Your questions are deep today, young lord," chuckled Julian. "You'd as leave ask how many angels can bathe in a thimble."

"What are you talking about?"

"Never mind. Some things must be taken on faith. But mark this; Iosa *will* work miracles in your life."

There was no denying it: miracles abounded. In fact, Evan's life had been one long succession of miracles beginning with Julian Antony Vorenius who had brought him Iosa's Truth, mentored and trained him, prepared him for everything he had faced since. The tiger that had nearly killed him, Augustus Claes, the giant Dungal, the Glamorth--all these things betrayed the presence of a complicated plan, the weaving together of a fabric that was more than the warp and weft of its parts. Even the terrible wounds he had suffered in Westerfeld had been part of the plan, just as his Watcher had suggested. Had he not been crippled, Phillipus would never have encouraged him to hold vigil in the church, and had he not been in the church Osric would be dead and Robert Fitzwarren on the throne.

Then, amidst the pictures and thoughts that mingled in his mind, another tangled tapestry began to form; of charred bodies in the smoldering remains of burned out buildings and people huddled together in fear. The leering face of the Red Goblin Klabaga was part of the weave too, but beyond that a broader darkness grew, and Evan knew he must find it before everything went midnight.

Above them, Julian circled and watched, sometimes ranging far ahead to spy out the best route or uncover hazards that the others couldn't see from the ground. The Watcher reflected on how fortunate he was to be a bird. Had they all been birds they would have long ago been in Faltigern. He wished they would hurry. Still, he would see them to Faltigern, however long that might take, and then he had business elsewhere.

He hadn't known about this business very long. A still, small voice had whispered to him during the night. In the north, someone needed a shove in the right direction and though it was certain to be a huge bother, one didn't lightly disobey the Creator of the Universe. Of course, humans did it all the time, but what would one expect? All he knew was that after Faltigern, he would fly north.

Below, Evan was praying again. Right now he was praying for the Clumsy Boy.

The Clumsy Boy didn't wake until the sun was well up in the sky. Waking proved the simple part. Movement elicited such pain from so many places that he was loathe to move again.

Eventually he managed to crawl up from the river into the shade of the trees where he tried to determine the extent of his injuries. If the pain was any indication, he had been killed. After a tentative examination he feared he might live.

Though bruised, cut, and scraped raw in dozens of places there were no broken bones. He was certain it was a miracle of some kind, but although thankful he had been spared, an encroaching fear began to overpower his gratitude. What was he going to do now?

He was on the wrong side of the river in a countryside swarming with hostile soldiers. Everything he owned had been lost to the river; his poniard was gone, his shoes were gone, most of his shirt was gone, the rest hanging in tatters from his narrow chest. Huge holes were worn in what remained of his trousers. He looked like a beggar who had taken a beating. He had no food, no money and few prospects.

He knew he was south of Durham near a small fishing village, but even if he managed to reach the settlement he was still in awful trouble. Convincing anyone that he was acting on behalf of the king's brother would be impossible in his present state. Still, the village was his only option.

Dusk had nearly fallen by the time he came upon what was left of the settlement. As he limped out of the trees, a gentle breeze carried the heavy smell of smoke and a far less pleasant odor. The failing light revealed many buildings that were but heaps of smoldering rubble, while others stood empty and dark. Nothing moved.

Martin crept nearer. Corpses lay in unnatural poses on the street. Carrion birds screeched in protest at the interruption of their gruesome meals. A stray dog barked and ran away. Why would anyone kill all these people? That was a woman. There, the body of a child. It was as though the entire human race had gone mad for blood and was racing to spill as much as they could before it was all gone.

Although there didn't appear to be anyone in the village that might help him, Martin was hungry enough to take a closer look. He approached the nearest intact structure.

The building was a warehouse of sorts, with four large doorways opening onto long wooden piers that extended out into the river. Broken barrels and smashed boxes littered the wharves and choked the doorways. Perhaps the looters had left something he could eat.

Batting at the flies that swarmed about him, he tripped over something near the doorway. It moved. It moaned.

Martin leapt back in horror, fell over his own feet and landed right beside the something in question. A hand closed about his arm.

"Water," hissed a weak voice, "Be a good lad and fetch me some water." The hand relaxed its grip.

Martin cried out and scuttled back like an awkward crab.

"Be quiet, will you?" said the voice. "Nobody can hear you but me and all I want is water. Please boy, fetch some water."

The voice sounded weaker than before. The boy came closer. "Who are you?" he whispered.

A pale face smeared with splashes of dried blood looked up with dark, hollow eyes.

"Please boy, a little water. Just a sip before I die."

Martin scurried away, returning with the remains of a broken pot in his hands. "Here's water sir," he said.

"Ah, there's a good lad." The stranger drank, closed his eyes and sighed.

"Are you hurt, sir?" ventured Martin.

The figure grunted. "I'm killed, boy. Killed by Duke Laighan's henchmen. Why should they want me dead? Why would they destroy this village? They've gone mad."

Blood caked around a vicious rent in the man's maille corselet. He wore the uniform of the Border Legion, though there were no Legion camps or detachments anywhere near Durham.

"How did the soldiers miss you?" the legionary asked in a voice that rattled and caught in his throat.

"I'm not from this village, sir," replied Martin, "I'm from the household of the King."

The soldier opened his eyes. "I'm dying and you tell me filthy lies. If I could move I'd teach you what for!"

"I'm not lying!" declared Martin and told the legionary how he had come to be there.

The wounded man clutched at Martin's collar. "May the flesh be stripped from your bones if you've played me false, but there's nothing else for it. It's either you or no one at all."

"What are you saying, sir? Shall I bring more water?"

"Just listen! I came from Gwenferew with a message for the King. But yesterday I ran across the Duke's friendly fellows who chased me to this poor place. There was a fight and this is all that's left of the town--and me." He fell silent again.

"But here's the point," he said presently. "They didn't get the King's message. Now you've got to deliver it."

Martin tried to pull away. "But I can't, don't you see? I told you what's happening in Durham. They're killing everyone!"

"Then stay alive," breathed the soldier, "and get this to the King."

He pulled a small bundle of cloth out of his cloak and held it out to Martin. "Tell my Centurion I did my best."

"Didn't you hear me? I can't go to Durham! Are you listening?"

But the legionary wasn't listening to anything anymore. Only his final imperative remained.

"Get this to the King."

Martin flopped down in the middle of the room. What next? None of this would have happened if he hadn't gone over the falls or if he had come to the warehouse just five minutes later.

And then he stopped in mid thought. Everything that had occurred since he left the palace had led him to this precise moment and this exact place. The same magnificent God that had saved him in the river had brought him here to complete the legionary's task.

As he rose to his knees, a grim determination replaced his fear. "I will not fail Thee, Lord."

And so, without a plan of any sort, Martin turned toward Durham. With him he took the sword of the dead legionary whose name he had never known, and the mysterious package to which the Lord of Hosts had led him.

———————

They rode until one of their horses foundered and then proceeded on foot leading the remaining mounts. No one spoke, each lost in private musings.

Eowulf's memories carried him back to a banquet where he had first heard Aine Ceallaigh sing. Her beauty had been breathtaking, and even now her magnificence remained untarnished despite her tangled hair and the ugly purple bruise across one cheek. He cringed. He wished he hadn't hurt her. No one should ever hurt her.

Beyond mere physical beauty, Aine Ceallaigh possessed a tangible air of dignity and poise that made her all the more alluring. And those eyes! One could be lost forever in those magnificent orbs of crystal blue. They shone like liquid fire. The longing in Eowulf's heart grew. He could forget the ruin of his life if only she would look upon him with favor.

Gauging the situation moment by moment, Aine watched Eowulf out of the corner of one eye.

She held her raw emotions in check only by the narrowest margin. What did they intend to do with her? She had overheard the priests whispering among themselves and seen Claranides staring at her with those dark, fathomless eyes. So she turned to her only possible source of help.

"What will you do with me?" she asked quietly.

Eowulf jerked as if suddenly awakened from a deep sleep. A twitch of confusion contorted his face before becoming a weak smile. "I don't know. I . . . I won't hurt you though."

Aine resisted a sarcastic reply. "Then let me go," she said.

Eowulf shook his head. "You'll get used to me in time."

"And if I don't? Why did you take me if you've no idea what you're going to do?"

"I took what I could get."

"But why do you want me?"

"You know," he replied sulkily. Was she taunting him?

"Ransom? My father can't pay much. If you returned home you'd have more gold than you could get from my father.

"What are you talking about? You know I can't go home!"

"How would I know that? You drag me out into the wild without so much as a by your leave and I'm supposed to know what's going on? The whole world has gone mad is all that I know!"

Eowulf glared at her, but felt compelled to explain everything that had befallen him. By the time he was done his anger had reached ferocious proportions and he expected Aine to rejoice at his incompetence, to taunt him for his failure. But Aine's response drained away his rage and left him feeling like a frightened boy.

"We have lost much, you and I," she said softly. "We are both at the mercy of someone else."

"I'm not at anyone's mercy!" Eowulf insisted.

"The priests," said Aine as though sharing a special secret. "Who knows what they will want from you."

"They won't get anything from me," Eowulf declared, trying to sound more certain than he felt. But the girl was right. Claranides would require something of him before it was all over.

"Will you not let me go?" Aine asked again.

"No I won't!"

Aine nodded as though accepting his answer. "Then tell me why you took me in the first place. What am I to you that you would do this thing?"

Eowulf hesitated, struggling against the chaos of his overwhelming passion.

"Is it because you're fond of me?" Aine asked as though astonished by the thought.

Eowulf blushed. He had never met a woman like Aine Ceallaigh. "Of course I'm fond of you. Do you think I took you for a hostage?" he snorted, shame rising around him.

"I am cross with you Eowulf Fitzwarren, for all the mischief you've done, but I'm glad you are fond of me."

"You are?"

"Yes. Because now I know you will keep your promise."

"What promise?"

"You promised not to hurt me. You gave your word, and I will hold you to it."

Eowulf nodded. "You'll be safe," he said, and although he wasn't certain he could control himself, Aine's safety had become his most pressing concern.

Despite their pace, it took nearly five days for the Priests and Eowulf to reach the rocky shores of Loch Aiden. They turned onto a trail that ended in a cluster of huts near a small, pebble-covered beach. Several small boats were drawn up on the shore where fishermen had spread nets to dry in the last rays of the setting sun.

Within moments they had secured passage on one of those boats. The boatman wasn't thrilled to be setting off across the lake so close to nightfall, but the Priesthood always paid well for service, especially since they were no longer welcome anywhere in the kingdom.

Secured to the mast by a length of stout rope, Aine closed her eyes on the dim horizon. In the comforting silence of the lake broken only by the gentle creak of the boat and the gurgle of the water, her thoughts wandered. She pictured Anwend Halfdane holding the gate. She imagined Evan, his health restored, driving Claranides and his brigands from the church. Evan, taking her in powerful arms and kissing her soundly. Evan.

How she loved him! In her youth she had often discussed love with other girls. She admired the stories, poems and songs that spoke the undying devotion and terrible sacrifices made by desperate lovers. Yet nothing she had heard or read or sung could express the emotion that welled in her heart when she thought of Evan MacKeth.

"Evan," she whispered.

She slept.

———

Aine woke to a light so intense that it took her breath away. It reflected from the surrounding water in shimmering rainbows and sharp darts of twinkling color like a gem so bright that it was impossible to look upon.

"Fiona's Lamp!" the boatman complained. "Curse of the Loch!"

The light leapt from the sky in a mad dance of brilliance, but the beauty and magic of the legend captivated only Aine, and for a few moments the passengers were forced to avert their eyes. Then the boat shuddered, heeled dangerously to starboard and rolled over.

Aine barely had time to cry out before she was submerged as the boat careened off the hidden rock. But as the others went overboard, the craft righted itself leaving Aine still lashed to the mast.

Encumbered by his maille and weapons Eowulf sank like a stone, but he was quick and agile, and before the weight could drag him to the bottom he struggled free of the armor and fought his way to the surface.

The current had done strange things. Two of the priests were nearly to the shore some hundred yards away while others thrashed at the water in a desperate attempt to stay afloat. But all of Eowulf's attention was drawn to Aine. The boat was sinking.

He swam after the damaged craft as it settled lower in the water, but the treacherous current that pulled it farther into the lake somehow drew Eowulf in the opposite direction. Aine struggled to free herself. The boat was sinking!

"Biscuit!" Eowulf cried, and across the distance Aine's desperate eyes locked onto his. Water covered her.

Never in his tragic life had Eowulf felt so alone and afraid. But that loneliness and fear imbued his limbs with strength beyond their limits, and he struck out against the current once more. He surged past the clinging tide and dove beneath the swirling water that marked the sunken boat. The rippled surface stilled. The lake grew quiet as the last light from Fiona's Lamp danced for a moment on the surface and then disappeared.

Eowulf came up with a heaving gasp that filled his pounding lungs with air. His arms held a motionless Aine.

"Breathe, Biscuit," he pleaded. "Breathe curse your eyes! You made me break my promise! Why do you hate me so much?" He slapped her again and again.

Then she choked up a great deal of water, took a ragged breath and rested her head against Eowulf's chest.

"Biscuit!" he cried. "That's it, breathe! I had to hit you. . . to save you."

He struck out for shore, his progress marked by inches as the lake fought to keep its prize. When at last he struggled into the shallows and staggered up the beach, he was spent. He carefully laid Aine on the grass and collapsed beside her. Nearby, Claranides looked down on the pair like a bird of prey.

By the time Julian warned them of the horsemen, Evan, Brian and Padraigh were crossing a large open valley between two rows of low, rolling hills. They weren't halfway across when twenty riders burst out of the trees in pursuit. The Watcher turned to delay the enemy however he might, and the pursued made for a distant creek bed with all speed.

Were it not for Julian they would have been ridden down long before they reached their destination, but the horses didn't like the clawing, biting bird. They shied and bolted, throwing riders and scattering horses across the meadow. But a dozen or more thundered on, rapidly closing the gap.

When Evan and his companions reached the wash, they couldn't hear their own labored breathing for the rumble of hooves behind. There was neither time to calculate the depth of the ravine nor determine the best place to descend. Crashing through the bordering brush they launched themselves over the edge.

However necessary, it seemed a poor bargain when they plunged twenty feet to the bottom of the draw. They landed hard on the uneven slope and rolled down into the waterless, boulder-strewn channel.

Evan tried to get up at once, but the fall had nearly knocked him senseless. He staggered and fell as he struggled to gain his feet. Blood ran into his eyes from a deep gash on his head. Brian sat dazed against a large rock while Padraigh cursed his alarmingly crooked leg.

One of the pursuers came hurtling over the edge of the streambed, landing with a sickening thud amid the screams of the rider and the shriek of the horse. Soon the rim was crowded with armed men.

"We've got to move," gasped Evan. A spear glanced off a rock nearby. "They'll find a way down."

"Let them," hissed Padraigh, "What fools we were to think we could fly!"

"It was fly or perish."

"I've broken my leg from flying!"

Evan and Brian dragged Padraigh across the streambed. On the far side they discovered a tangle of large rocks and uprooted trees wedged together by the spring floods. Just as they wriggled into this makeshift fortress the riders appeared.

Evan shook the blood out of his eyes and sighted down the edge of his sword. Now that it had come down to steel, a terrible calm stole over him. It was simple, basic and final. Standing between Aine and him were these horsemen. He welcomed them.

They approached the barricade demanding immediate surrender. There was nothing to indicate whom these men served, but it was clear that they didn't intend to let the trio pass. After arguing the best course of action, the enemy dismounted and came at them from all sides.

For a few moments it was steel and shouts and blood. The attackers rushed up only to be sent reeling back. By the time they retired, one of their number lay dead and several others had to be carried away. But it had cost the defenders too. Brian grimaced from a nasty cut across his back while Padraigh, already in considerable pain from the broken leg, had been stabbed in the hand. They bandaged themselves as best they could and waited.

Julian flitted down and perched on a branch near Evan.

"Well?" said Evan as though expecting something.

"Well what?" countered the bird, casually preening his feathers.

"You missed the fight, so the least you can do is tell me what's going on out there."

Julian frowned but said nothing. He could fly away; his companions were trapped.

"How many did you see?"

"Too many," offered Julian, "You know I can't count. Lots."

Evan peered out to where their enemies were gathered. He counted sixteen. It was just as Julian said: too many.

"What now?" asked Brian.

Padraigh shrugged. "When it's dark, the two of you must get away and fetch help - if they don't burn us out first."

"What about you?"

"I'll keep these fellows busy."

"Let's have a look at that leg," suggested Evan. In a short time the broken bone had been set, splinted and secured with strips of cloth torn from their clothing.

There was another desultory skirmish before sunset, broken up almost entirely by the Watcher. If the practiced blades of the defenders weren't enough, the shrieking, clawing, biting bird tipped the balance. But even the remarkable bird wasn't immune to physical considerations and returned with a deep cut over one green eye. Amidst Julian's bad tempered complaints, Evan saw to the wound.

The boy scolded, "Be careful can't you? It's no good getting killed when I'm just beginning to get used to you."

"Foolish Boy," hummed the Watcher with pleasure, "you can't kill a Zalathrax so easily."

"No such thing as a Zalathrax," chided Evan.

At nightfall the enemy kindled a fire and cooked part of the dead horse. The tempting aroma made Evan's mouth water and put everyone in a bad mood, but the idea of a sortie to get at the food was abandoned.

They waited. The night sky was clear and scattered with stars, as though some mystic giant had thrown handfuls of silver into the heavens. The moon, low and bright, cast so much illumination that escape seemed impossible. They waited and slept in turns.

The horsemen made no move against them. Eventually the fire died away to embers and the sounds from the camp gave way to the gentle silence of the cool night air and the haloed light of moon and stars.

Julian cocked his head to one side and blinked at Evan with his one good eye. The other had swollen shut.

"Time?" he whispered. "Time to go?"

"Aye. Time to go."

Padraigh nodded.

Evan turned back to Julian.

"Be careful," he warned, stroking the sleek feathers on Julian's breast. "I'll see you in Faltigern."

"You'll see me," chirped the Watcher, "when you least expect me." Julian flew away.

In a few moments the sound of panicked horses and alarm erupted from the enemy camp, but far from the simple diversion the Watcher was intended to provide, the fray erupted into a full-scale battle. The night echoed with screams and curses. Evan and Brian clambered out of their warren only to be forced back by a swarm of riders.

"Best come out," urged a voice. "Better to hang than burn."

"It'll be unpleasant for you if we come out," warned Brian.

"Suit yourself! Bring a torch!"

Padraigh laughed. "Ferghal MacMorris! Be polite to my companions or I'll put you in the stocks myself! The king's brother is standing right beside me!"

"Padraigh? Sir Rinn? What are you doing in there?"

"Just pull me out! 'Ware my leg!"

Once free of the tangled branches, Padraigh found himself surrounded by the men of Duke Eiolowen's fief.

"You're a welcome sight," Padraigh exclaimed, "but whatever are you doing in this lonely place?"

"Those fellows over there," Ferghal replied, gesturing to the little band of prisoners his men had taken. "They've been gathering along the borders of the fief, but tonight they crossed onto our land. I suspect they serve Duke Ringan, though why he'd send armed men against us I've no idea."

Padraigh explained what was happening in Durham and what he had been sent to accomplish. "Get me to the castle. The future of Glenmara rests with us."

In moments they were galloping eastward, leaving the bodies of their prisoners hanging from nearby trees. Of the Watcher there was no sign.

―――――

Aine opened her eyes, reluctant to emerge from the comfort of oblivion. She found herself lying at the head of a broad valley that stretched out toward the looming peaks of the snow-capped Balinora Mountains. Atop a distant plateau an elaborate building of golden stone commanded the landscape. Even the intervening miles couldn't diminish the splendor of the structure, and Aine found herself drawn to it. But as her mind cleared, she remembered the events that had brought her to this place. She relived the helpless horror of being tied to the sinking boat and the cold finality of the water closing over her head. She sobbed.

"There, there Biscuit," soothed Eowulf's rough voice, "Don't cry. You're safe."

Through tears she looked up into the anxious, searching eyes of her abductor. "I might have died," she said, "because you cannot control your passions." Had she struck him it could have caused no greater pain.

"But you didn't die," he replied as though apologizing. "I saved you."

"Saved me? To what end? That you may dishonor me at your leisure? To serve the designs of the priests? You'd as leave have let me drown!"

Eowulf's voice trembled. "It wasn't my fault the boat sank! That stupid fisherman ran us onto a rock. It wasn't my fault you nearly drowned!"

"Who tied me to the mast?" demanded the girl, anger overcoming the terror of her remembrance.

"You'd have run else wise."

"And why shouldn't I run? Do you suppose to kidnap me and receive a smile in kind? You nearly drown me and expect thanks? It's only by God's grace that I'm even alive!"

"I saved you," growled Eowulf, "not God!"

Aine stood. "Should I thank the mighty Eowulf for his protection?" she hissed, and he stepped back from the menace in her eyes. "Would you have me thank you for the misery and sorrow you've caused? Answer me!"

"Don't push me Biscuit," he seethed. "You're trying to make me break my word, aren't you? They were all like you. They pushed too. Where do you suppose they are now?" He glared at her, looking for a final provocation that would allow him to crush her. But there was a terrible fear in his dark eyes, the dismal, darting look of a starving wolf that knows it is death to take the bait, yet driven by an insatiable hunger.

Aine turned away, still weeping. She might have pitied Eowulf were he not so dangerous. She could only imagine what horrible things had molded him, not that it would make any difference if she knew.

Gentle hands caressed her shoulders.

Eowulf whispered, "Don't cry Biscuit. I'll take care of you."

She shuddered. There was more rage and passion in Eowulf Fitzwarren than she could ever hope to control. Eventually he would turn on her. In the distance the spires of Moloch's Temple gleamed like golden teeth in the afternoon sun.

———————

They arrived at the temple as the last light of day disappeared beyond the western horizon. Long before they reached the plateau they were intercepted by a party of armed men who escorted them up the winding approach to the top of the ridge. On either side of the narrow, zigzag road, an encampment filled with tents and hard looking men covered the slope.

Aine had heard stories and descriptions of the Great Temple, but none of them approached the glory of seeing the structure in person. From a distance, the wall surrounding the temple compound appeared but a simple protective structure, but as they drew near it became apparent that the entire stone surface was one continuous carving of intricate designs inlaid with filigree of copper and bronze. The light from the setting sun gave the stone the disturbing appearance of movement as shadows danced across the wall.

But if the walls were remarkable, the bracing towers were epic in their grotesque magnificence. Each of the seven turrets lining the western edge of the plateau had been constructed in the image of fantastic mythical beasts. They towered above the valley like terrifying sentinels, human bodies with the heads of bears and fish and birds. The central figure, however, chilled Aine's blood with unholy dread.

Bracing the wide gateway, massive stone legs rose above the wall to merge with torso, arms and the gigantic head and horns of a ram. Sheathed in plates of beaten bronze, this figure overshadowed the others in size and intricacy of detail. Gems the size of wagon wheels stared down at them from the eye sockets of the colossus.

Aine shuddered as they passed through the gate. "Thou shalt make unto thee no graven images," she whispered.

The interior of the compound spread out to the edges of the ridge and back to the first rocky slopes of the Balinora range. Dozens of buildings and structures covered the finely manicured grounds, bordered by carefully groomed trees and festive gardens, but these, though well kept and pleasing to the eye, were insignificant beside the temple itself.

Rising from the center of the plateau to a height surpassing even the gateway statue stood a pyramid of black rock veined with golden tracery. Broad steps mounted to a doorway over which stood yet another image of Moloch fashioned from solid gold.

There was great excitement and concern at the return of Claranides, and Aine found it amusing to see the startled expressions of the clerics gathered around him. Her amusement turned to ice and melted in a sudden surge of fear when Claranides turned his cold eyes upon her.

"Take her," the High Priest said, and a dozen strong hands seized Aine. Before Eowulf could intervene, he too was wrestled down.

Now, alone in a well-appointed room, Aine tried not to imagine what they intended to do with her. Her captors had at least provided good food and a warm scented bath, but she had the unmistakable feeling she was being watched. She ate, but decided to wait on the bath.

From an adjoining room, several individuals observed her with great interest.

"Those bruises must heal," lamented one.

"There's time for that," assured another, "We'll make time. What the master has in mind requires a perfect sacrifice."

"How long?"

"A week, perhaps two."

"Much can happen in two weeks . . ."

"Don't worry. However long it takes, Moloch will prevail. The blood of Aine Ceallaigh will see to that."

———

In a dark chamber in the bowels of the pyramid, Eowulf struggled until he was exhausted and weeping from anger and frustration. Those cursed priests had taken the only thing he had, his Biscuit. She had warned him they would require something and he hadn't listened. He had failed her, and now had killed himself in the bargain.

Yet death was inconsequential; after all that had happened it would be a relief. He had broken so many promises to so many people throughout his life, and more than anything else he wanted to keep his promise to Aine. The thought of failing drove his rage beyond reason.

He twisted and pulled until the blood pounded in his head, and his wrists were torn and bloody from the ropes. On the edge of madness, with a final violent effort, his hands slid free of the blood soaked cords.

Eowulf crouched in the darkness and fondled the small knife his captors had failed to take from his boot. Taking stock of his surroundings he began to plan an escape.

CHAPTER IV
CHANGING DIRECTIONS

On the morning of the fifth day of the siege at Durham, a small boat drifted close enough to the castle dock to be recovered by the defenders. Inside they discovered the battered bodies of three women and a child. Nothing would have come of this discovery had they not also fished something out of the river.

Tangled in a rope trailing from the stern of the partially submerged craft, soldiers discovered a most curious creature. It had apparently been in the water for a long time, but surely the river couldn't make a body look like that! It was fat and round with short stubby legs, long spindly arms and pale, slate grey skin. The stench was so horrendous that only curiosity prevented them throwing it back. What was it?

So, despite the smell, they kept it and eventually managed to entice Torgal the Terrible to have a look. He examined the body at great length, poked and pulled and finally ordered it brought to his tower.

"Is it the Water Dragon, Master Torgal?" inquired one of the soldiers.

"Ain't there a reward fer it?" asked another.

"It's not the Water Dragon," Torgal answered as he directed the removal of the strange body. "It's a goblin."

"What's a goblin doing in the river?"

"An excellent question."

When Torgal had completed the examination of the corpse he invited the king to view the curiosity, but Osric had no time to spend on curiosities.

"So how do you suppose a Grey Goblin wound up in the river?" Osric asked just to be polite.

Torgal was beside himself with excitement. "I cannot say, majesty. The headwaters of the Cuinn originate in the northern mountains. I would assume the goblin came from there, somewhere in the north."

"Goblins floating down the river! What next?" Osric cried.

———————

Farming, fishing and forestry made Faltigern a thriving city. Supported by the teeming waters of Loch Aiden, the lush forests and the rich agricultural lands surrounding, it was an active center of trade. Now, in the week of Spring Festival, the eastern settlement swarmed with people and animals, the extra population overflowing the city to claim every vacant space and plot of ground within a mile of the town.

Past the throngs of people, through the parades and celebration, Evan and Brian made for the headquarters of the Provisional Militia housed in the old Legion barracks on the far side of town. Like Gwenferew, Faltigern had once been a Legion town, but as the city grew, the Legion garrison was displaced to a fortress across the loch. The protection of Faltigern was now the duty of the Militia.

More than a thousand men served with the Provisional Militia, supported by a yearly subscription that paid to train, equip and sustain Faltigern's own private army. Officers and enlisted alike drew pay for every day spent in training or on campaign. The Faltigern Provisional Militia was the best trained, most highly regarded unit of its kind in Glenmara.

Brought before Commander Lothar Mohdru, Evan presented documents calling for the muster of the Militia into the king's service. They were ordered to proceed with all dispatch to Cardiff Eoilowen and place themselves under the command of Sir Padraigh Rinn.

Lothar called for his orderly. "Will you accompany us, lord?" he asked Evan.

"No. We've business with the Legion. We need a boat."

"And you shall have it!" Lothar declared.

Events were speeding up now, rushing madly toward the uncertain future, and Evan was glad of it. The boat pulled out onto the lake past hundreds of other craft. The sails filled with wind and the sleek little vessel heeled gracefully as it sped across the water. Exhausted, Brian and Evan fell to the deck. The last thing that crossed Evan's mind before sleep overwhelmed him was a question; where *was* Julian?

———————

Far above the earth the Watcher floated lazily along, wafted by the gentle winds that carried him for miles without requiring he even flap a wing. Being a bird, he loved to fly, but now he regarded even that in a different light. Now his thoughts were beyond birdish concerns, dwelling on matters more lofty than ever a bird had visited before, and he reflected that the joy of flying at such "lofty" altitudes and the idea of "lofty" matters was an altogether appropriate mixture.

He didn't know what he was doing. Not that he was unaware of his destination or of what he was supposed to accomplish once he got there, but he didn't understand why it was more important than keeping an eye on the Foolish Boy. After all, only God knew what sort of mischief Evan might get into without his Watcher.

Yet that was the point; God knew. He knew everything, so there was nothing to worry about. There was only to do as he was told.

And so he would. He would fly north though he knew Evan was about to face a terrible choice. He wished he could be there to nudge him in the right direction.

"God will take care of the details," he sighed, and turning a loop in the cool, clear sky he flew north.

Evan woke with a jolt. He gasped, sat up and tried to catch his breath. Brian still slept beside him while the ship's crew went about their various tasks as though the two passengers weren't even there. It wasn't the movement of the ship, nor the actions of the sailors, nor the cries of the lake birds, nor even his own dreams that woke him. Instead it was the sudden, incontrovertible knowledge that he was going the wrong way.

He scrambled to the railing and stared out over the water toward the distant Balinora Mountains. The Hinnom Valley was there, Aine was there, his future and any hope for happiness was there, but he couldn't see the mountains or Aine or the future for the vision that filled his head. Somewhere thousands of corpses covered a rolling meadow. Somewhere a Red Goblin named Klabaga waited for him--somewhere in the north.

The young warrior slumped to the deck. There was no mistaking it; he had been *called*. Just as he had been summoned to face the Glamorth in the dark caverns of Westerfeld, now God was sending him to face the Red Goblin and the evil he brought with him. He shook his head as if to dislodge the realization from his mind. Anger overcame him.

"How can You ask this of me?" he whispered, and then aloud added, "Lord, how can You ask this of me?"

Sailors glanced nervously about.

"Surely this can wait a day or two! We're almost there."

Evan hadn't bargained for this. Iosa had healed him, delivered him from the hands of Claranides, but what mercy was any of that if He took Aine away?

"I won't do it!" he growled, tears springing to his eyes. "Anything else, but not this. I won't do it!"

"Who are you arguing with?" grumbled Brian.

Evan didn't answer. "Ask something else!" he demanded, moving away from his companion. "I can't give You what You want."

But the pictures in his head intensified. Horrific images of terror, blood and fear flashed before his eyes, and he knew that this was only the beginning. The pure essence of evil was coming to the world, bringing war, famine and disease in its wake. What was beginning in Glenmara would spread to devour the entire world.

The words of Julian Antony Vorenius leapt into his mind with frightening clarity: *They're out there. They still plot and plan and scheme. One day they will rise up and spread across the world like an ugly stain of blood.*

For the first time Evan began to grasp why he was a Warrior of the Son, why such warriors even existed. Thirty years ago Julian had driven the darkness back into Sheol. Now it was crawling up from the Pit again and Evan had been called to stand in the breach.

He wept. The elation of giving himself to Iosa Christus, the wonder of his triumph over the Glamorth, the miracle of his healing seemed to fade into insignificance without Aine. She wasn't supposed to be part of the bargain.

Words from The Book danced through his tortured mind. "*if you ask your Father for bread, will he give you a stone?*" It felt like a stone. "*Seek first His kingdom and His righteousness and all these things will be added unto you.*" He believed these words. The truth of these words had saved him again and again. But how could his desire to rescue Aine be contrary to God's plan? Hadn't God brought them together in the first place?

Evan tore at his clothing. He was so consumed with despair that he didn't notice they had drawn abreast of the Legion fortress. He didn't hear the challenge from the walls or the reply from the boat, and he was unaware when they docked at the quay. He knew nothing other than the torment in his heart and the mad thoughts racing through his mind until Brian shook him by the shoulders.

"Wake up! We're here. You've got the documents, don't you?"

Evan followed Brian onto the dock. He met Tribune Galba, the commander of the small Legion detachment, and delivered the parchment letter sealed by the High King himself. Information was exchanged, food and drink brought. All this, and yet to Evan it was as if he weren't there. He spoke, he breathed, he moved, but his spirit was somewhere far away, fighting against the will of God.

"Kidnapped the young Lady, did they?" snarled Tribune Galba, "What a treacherous lot! Overthrow the crown? On my oath there will be a reckoning!"

"There are two thousand soldiers guarding the Temple, plus three hundred of Moloch's assassins," mentioned Galba's Centurion. "The Priesthood has built quite an army since they were exiled."

Galba waved his hand. "Mercenaries can't match legionaries. With two hundred of the Second's finest at our command, even the Inquisitors shouldn't cause us much problem. We'll get Lady Ceallaigh back, Lord MacKeth. Never you fear."

The legionaries prepared for the field. Word quickly spread that they were marching to the temple to recover something valuable. Ahead of them lay a long walk and a hard fight; genuine enthusiasm resulted.

Evan wasn't among the enthusiastic. He was glad they were going to rescue Aine, but if he were to accompany them he would have to disobey God.

"What's the matter with you?" asked Brian as he downed a bowl of steaming Legion porridge. "Have you been struck in the head?"

"I'm just anxious to be off," snarled Evan.

If they moved quickly he could do God's bidding with only a slight delay. It would be all right. He wasn't disobeying, just postponing. Iosa would understand. Wouldn't He?

He watched the legionaries clattering about in the fortress yard. Centurions bellowed commands,

Optios checked equipment and pushed men into line. The Tribune had promised they would be ready to march by dusk, but even so it would take two days to reach the temple. Two days there, a day, perhaps two to complete the rescue and two days back--nearly a week. Scarcely a slight delay.

Evan turned from the battlements toward a horizon marked by bands of dark, angry clouds. The world had gone mad. Glenmara convulsed in the throes of a civil war that would spread across the entire kingdom. Every man, woman and child would pay a price for the greed and ambition of Duke Robert Fitzwarren. Now appeared the Red Goblin, a meadow full of corpses, and evil crawling up from the bowels of the earth.

His decision would define the remainder of his life. What was his future worth if he disobeyed God? Of what purpose the lessons taught by Julian Antony Vorenius if he strayed from the path now?

His mind raced toward an unsettling understanding. In the dark shadow of Westerfeld when he had looked into the hideous yellow eyes of Klabaga, he believed they would meet again. He now realized that by destroying the Glamorth he had already affected the plans of the Red Goblin.

It was all connected. Everything that had happened to him since childhood was part of a greater mechanism designed to bring him to this moment. Had Evan not destroyed the Glamorth, the unseen peril would be greater still. Had he not been injured so deeply he wouldn't have held vigil in the chapel, where he had saved his brother and thwarted the plans of the priests. Had Aine not been kidnapped he would have never left Osric's side and would not now be free to go about the Will of Iosa Christus.

Nothing was set in stone. Anything might change everything. The decision was his, yet there was no doubt what was expected of him.

He shook his fist at the sky. "I never asked to be a Warrior of the Son. I just want Aine! But You must know that. I'll go where You send me, but sweet mercy, the timing of it!"

Evan trembled from the impact of his decision. The vision of Aine's beauty and the remembrance of their first kiss tore at his resolve.

"You save her then," he demanded. "I place her in Your care. I'm giving her up! That's what You want isn't it?"

Evan approached Brian. "I can't go with you," he blurted out.

Brian's eyes narrowed. "What are you talking about? What do you mean you can't go?"

"I've been called . . . by God. There's something I've got to do. There." He pointed vaguely toward the lake.

"God? What rubbish!"

Evan's anger flared. "What do you know about it? Something bad is happening . . ."

"Be certain something bad is happening. In Durham. At Moloch's temple. We'll long for peace before this business is done. But don't use God to excuse your cowardice!"

Sacred suffering saints! This is what You want, isn't it? "Think what you like," Evan hissed, laying hand to sword. "Just rescue her, curse you! That's your job now; bring her back."

"That I will!"

Evan stood rigid as Brian walked away. The Legion was nearly ready to march. The boat was almost ready to set sail. He took one final look at the mountains, and then sadly turned west toward his destiny.

———————

The terror Martin had experienced in the river was nothing compared to the fear that gripped him now. By stealth and good fortune he had managed to sneak back into Durham, but the town was full of soldiers and his plan to reenter the palace grew more perilous with every step.

If only he could get to the river! He surveyed the forbidding street from the ruins of a burned out building. He had often been into the town to visit the apothecary or explore the varied excitements of the market, and had traveled this street many times. But tonight it was deserted and dark, like the road to a graveyard. It was only a few blocks to the river, less than a hundred yards, but even if he managed to reach it, his journey was far from over, and if he were discovered . . .

He scrambled down a mound of debris into the basement and crawled into a corner. He would never get into the palace. The Sceir Naid might have been on the moon and he had just as much likelihood of reaching that distant orb as ever setting foot in the palace again. He was hungry. He was frightened. He was tired. He slept.

Dreams, when they came, were filled with strange, whispered voices in an indecipherable language. Eventually they changed from hushed, elusive tones to urgent, strident argument, and suddenly burst forth into the ancient language of Ascalon, the Common Language that bound the world together. Now the dream began to make sense.

"If you don't stop speaking Varangian you'll get us all killed!"

"It wasn't my fault those fellows didn't like foreigners. And we made 'em pay for meddling!"

"We paid too. Some of us aren't here anymore."

"It's war. What'd you expect? Is Otho afraid of dying?"

"No," retorted Otho, "but he's not in any itching hurry for it either. If I'm going to die it'll be at Lord Halfdane's side, not in some fool of a fight you've started, Ragnar!"

"He's right," said another voice. "You're as wild a Berserk as your father ever was."

"What of it? There's nothing wrong with being like your Da. Who'll say something bad about my Da?"

"You want to fight us now?"

"Come on little man! Dance with Ragnar!"

Something thudded heavily against the basement wall. Martin woke up.

"In Odin's name isn't there enough trouble without we kill each other? Otho, Ragnar, calm down or I'll split your heads!"

"You're not chieftain, Aethelred."

"True enough, but until we can get to Lord Halfdane, I'm in charge. Dispute that and you'll have your fight."

Martin's fear evaporated. If he could get to Anwend Halfdane's Varangians he could go anywhere.

He climbed up to the street and found his way into the adjacent building. In its dark, deserted confines, his footfalls echoed like drumbeats. A stairway beckoned. The anxious boy took one step, slipped on the smooth wooden runner and tumbled headlong into the abyss.

He slammed to an abrupt halt against the unyielding dirt floor, and before he could catch his breath or determine if he had killed himself, he was seized up and thrust hard against the brick wall. Dim candlelight glimmed on maille and cast shadows across grim faces framed by braided hair and beards.

"Hvem er du?" demanded the large fellow who held Martin suspended off the floor with one gigantic hand.

Martin gasped for breath. "What?"

Someone pressed the point of a sword against the boy's belly. "He asked who you are. Be quick with an answer!"

"I . . . I'm Martin Reamon, servant to Lord Evan MacKeth," the boy blurted out. "I've come to take you to Lord Halfdane!"

"The likes of you knows Lord Halfdane? You've told your last lie, beggar boy."

"I'm not lying! I was there when he defended the gate! I was there when the king embraced him!"

"The gate? The king? What are you talking about?"

"He held the gate against twenty men! Alone!" enthused Martin. "But for him the kingdom would have fallen and the king been slain!"

"What are you saying?"

"Aren't you listening? He held the gate. He was wounded . . ."

"Wounded?" cried someone. The hand that held Martin's tunic twisted the fabric until he was choking.

"Not badly! I'll take you to him. Let me go!"

"Release him, Ragnar. Tell us about the gate, beggar boy."

Martin told them all he knew, and when he was done, the Varangians responded with violent enthusiasm.

"Our Lord held the gate!"

"By Thor's Hammer we've got to get to him!"

"Let's go!"

Several men started up the stairs.

"Where are you going?" demanded Aethelred. "You'll never get into the palace. We can't help Lord Halfdane if we're dead."

"What do you suggest? Sit here like so many moles in the ground?" snarled Ragnar.

Martin chimed in. "I told you, I'll take you there myself. I'm going there anyway."

"And how will you manage that?"

Once Martin outlined his plan, thirty-two hardened Varangian warriors were ready to follow a beardless youth. They declared that Thor the Thunder God had sent the boy to take them where they might die beside their Master. Martin didn't know anything about Thor, but he was certain that it had been Lord Evan's God, the God of Heaven and Earth and of thunder too, Who had brought him here.

And so, just as he had gone out, Martin got back into the palace, leading his own small army. "I must see the king!" he demanded of the startled guards.

"Where did you come from? Who are all these big fellows with you?"

"I must deliver this message to the king," Martin insisted.

"Nobody's going anywhere until I get some answers! Owen, fetch the Captain of the Guard. We've got unexpected visitors."

Once notified, Osric ordered Martin brought before him. Notwithstanding the boy's appearance and the attendant stench from his trip through the sewer, the king was anxious to see him.

"How have you returned to us, brave Martin?" Osric asked. He pressed a goblet into the boy's hand and Martin drained it. "My brother. Tell me of Evan."

Martin told his story and when he was finished, he delivered the package from the dead legionary. Osric opened the parcel and stared in fascinated revulsion at the contents. A letter spoke of dead legionaries and strange fingers found beneath a rock. The simple communication asked nothing, conveyed little and didn't appear to have any bearing on what was happening in Durham, yet something about the strange decomposing finger tickled at the back of Osric's mind. Something Torgal had said; something about the thing they had fished out of the river.

"You're a remarkable boy," said the king, "and your bravery will be rewarded. Now clean yourself up and get something to eat. We shall have need of your strength and cunning."

When the boy had gone, Osric summoned Torgal and shared the grotesque treasure. Comparing it to the hand of the creature in Torgal's study, it was apparent the finger had come from a goblin hand. The king's mood darkened.

Long before Osric's birth, in the time of his father and grandfather, the wide world had been engulfed in the great war against Sheol. Some called it the Demon Wars, others the War of Shadow. During those dreadful years massive armies of goblins and trolls led by dark, fell spirits swarmed across the countries to the west. Such were the stories and legends of those dim, distant times, though no one spoke about them now.

With the fabric of their lives already hanging in tatters, this was a possibility more ominous than anything they faced. But whatever was happening beyond the palace walls would have to wait.

Bathed, groomed, and with new clothing, Martin was escorted to the kitchens for a meal.

"There he is!" exclaimed a familiar voice and before he could take another step he was pulled into an adjoining room where his Varangian companions dined. They cleared a place at table, shoved him onto the bench and thrust a trencher, mounded high with meat and cheese, in front of him.

"So this is the fellow who brought my wayward children home?" Anwend Halfdane enthused. "I will reward you."

"Thank you, Lord," Martin grumbled through a mouthful of mutton, "but it isn't necessary."

The Varangians howled and hooted.

"Not necessary? Not necessary?" Ragnar spouted.

Aethelred threatened. "Lord Halfdane decides what's necessary, youngster."

"As you say! I shall humbly accept any reward offered."

"Gone mercenary now, is it?"

"Greedy little beggar boy!"

"I'm not a beggar boy!"

"He's no beggar boy," assured Gervald. "He's some sort of juggling scullery maid. But he'll fight too." He related his first encounter with Martin, and great was the merriment that followed the telling. They slapped their new friend across the back, tousled his hair and offered him more food and wine. The boy couldn't help but smile, even though he wasn't certain he was entirely safe in the company of such men.

"Well, whatever you are, my sword is yours," Anwend declared.

The Varangians surged to their feet scattering furniture and crockery across the room. "Our swords!" they cried, drawing steel to flash in the torchlight. "Our swords!"

Martin thought he would burst with pride.

———

As grim as the situation remained in Durham, it was worse in Gwenferew. Goblins searched every house, barn and shed for prisoners and plunder. From atop the watchtower in the Legion stockade, lookouts reported large war bands marching off in all directions across the countryside.

The chaos within the Legion compound had stabilized into a sort of organized madness. With the women and small children safely tucked away in various buildings, the remainder had been organized into manageable groups, armed with anything that might do damage to flesh, and assigned to the supervision of a senior legionary.

Many of the smaller structures in the camp were dismantled, their timbers stockpiled to repair any breach in the fortress wall. Legionaries were relieved in shifts for meals and rest. Water was plentiful since the Legion had its own well, but with so many extra mouths to feed, all foodstuffs and livestock were gathered together and placed under guard. Alcohol was confiscated to prevent drunkenness.

Tribune Ronan coordinated these activities with disciplined severity. In the absence of Giomer, Ronan had taken command as the senior Tribune, and though his orders were instantly obeyed, without the calming presence of their Commander, a quiet despair began to take root among the legionaries. Only the constant attention of the junior officers kept panic at bay.

Inside the town hall Optio Tyrus considered his options. His makeshift army had fought well, but after three vicious assaults and their own share of casualties, the endurance of the humans was reaching its limit. With neither the experience nor training of real soldiers, they were close to breaking.

There remained one hope--get to the Legion fortress if it still held. Tyrus was still trying to solidify the beginnings of a plan when the first stone crashed into an adjacent building on the west side of the plaza. Another melon-sized stone arched into the air and came down with a bang, shattering on the cobblestones.

The Optio raced to the roof where one of his legionaries stood watch.

"They're coming from over there," said the soldier pointing, "Those grey rats've got catapults."

As he strained to see beyond the plaza, Tyrus observed another missile arch up from behind a row of houses. It impacted on the fountain, destroying the central statuary in a spray of water and broken marble.

"So it seems," remarked the Optio, "but they're terrible shots."

With catapults the goblins would be able to reduce the building to ruins at their leisure. Tyrus called for Legionary Wren.

Gwenferew boasted a well-designed drainage system. Covered by heavy wooden gratings, shallow, stone-lined ditches crisscrossed the entire town. One of them came right into the town hall and led, theoretically at least, into the Legion fortress. Though too small for goblins, these ditches would accommodate little Wren. When Optio Tyrus had finished giving orders, Wren, The Bird, as he was known by his mates, lay aside his weapons, stripped off his armor, and squeezed into the evil smelling trench.

Outside darkness fell and the goblins continued to improve their aim.

———————

Braslav woke to find two large eyes staring at him. Neither friendly nor menacing, they were still eyes, and that was disconcerting enough. He waved his hand and snorted, "Shoo! Shoo!" but they remained unblinking, just two eyes in a dark corner of a Legion woodshed.

He sat up and growled, "Get out of here. This is my woodshed and not for the likes of you, whatever you are."

He had been drinking, though the bottle was empty now, and the wine had only made him sleepy. When the two eyes spoke to him, he suspected he was already drunk.

"I'm a bird," said the eyes in a soothing, strangely accented voice, "a Zalathrax. A Watcher."

"What're you doing watching me? Go watch somebody else. But watch out for more wine, can you?" laughed Braslav, certain he was hallucinating.

"You don't need any more wine," warned the eyes. "Listen carefully. I have a message for you."

"Look, I don't need a . . . a bird did you say? I don't need a bird telling me what to do. I won't stand for it! I've got to get more wine, and that's all there is to it. Before those grey fellows cut our throats I intend to be very drunk."

As he moved toward the doorway the eyes turned hard and full of fire. A horrible hissing filled the air. Braslav scrambled back against the woodpile as the eyes advanced, and their owner came into view.

It was indeed a bird behind those remarkable green eyes, though the eyes were no more remarkable than the remainder of the bird. Swathed in iridescent, purple-black feathers, it peered at Braslav along a beak edged with formidable teeth. Long talons clawed at the earthen floor while broad wings fanned the air.

"A talking bird? I've got to get more of that wine! What do you want anyway? Aren't there other birds you can talk to? Leave me alone!"

"Not before I deliver a message."

"A message? From whom?" demanded Braslav.

"From the One Who sends your dreams," replied the bird.

Braslav found it difficult to breathe. He gasped and pulled at his beard. "How do you know about my dreams?"

"I am a servant of He Who sends them."

"Who?"

"The One True God."

Braslav shook his head. "I don't know the One True God."

Julian pointed his wing at the man. "That's as may be, but He knows you."

Braslav bristled. "Why has He cursed me with these visions? I want to be ignorant like everyone else. They stumble around like a lot of sheep because they can't see it. But it's out there. It's coming and I can't get away!"

"Yes," the bird agreed, "It's coming."

"Why does this God hate me so?"

The Watcher smiled. "He isn't *this* god, He is *the* God, the One True God, the maker of all things, and He doesn't hate you. His love for you is beyond telling."

While Braslav cowered in the back of the shed, Julian delivered the message.

―――――――

It was intended as a simple sacrificial ceremony to prepare for the offering of Aine Ceallaigh. As a personal reward given by Claranides for loyal and devoted service, Phillipus recognized it as a significant gift. Eowulf Fitzwarren was of noble birth, and the god favored the blood of nobility.

Yet as he wended his way through the temple, past the icons, images and symbols of Moloch's power, Phillipus felt the remorseless gnawing of doubt. Despite the cunning, patience, and sacrifice of the priesthood, Moloch's power had failed against the power of Iosa Christus. All their careful plans had been brought to a crushing, useless end in the chapel on the Sceir Naid.

Phillipus knew their failure went beyond incompetence or the random alignment of fate. He suspected a lack of faith had ruined everything, if one dared use such words to describe anything associated with the High Priest. But everyone was talking about it. Word of the disaster had spread, and now a current of fear permeated the very air of the Temple. Now they would sacrifice again to expiate their guilt, and though he cursed himself for the thought, Phillipus wasn't certain it would be enough.

Eowulf was still on the cell floor where they had left him two days before, and it wasn't until the two attendants pulled the prisoner to his feet that they noticed he was no longer bound. By that time there was little they could do but scream as the knife did its work. Before Phillipus could react, he was hurled to the floor. Eyes ablaze with hatred, Eowulf pressed the bloody steel against the priest's cheek.

"Don't make a sound, or twitch a muscle, or have a thought, or you'll join your friends."

From the corner of his eye Phillipus saw the twitching bodies of his unfortunate subordinates.

"Are you listening to me, you treacherous dog?" Spittle flew from Eowulf's lips, and his whole body trembled. Phillipus nodded.

"Good. Now I'm going to tell you what to do, and then you're going to do it. Understand? No discussion, no questions. If I get the slightest hint of an argument out of you, if I don't like the look in your eyes, I'll kill you. Understand?"

Phillipus nodded again.

Eowulf bound the priest's wrists, retrieved a sword from one of the dead acolytes and pulled his prisoner close. "Remember, not a sound. Now take me to Aine Ceallaigh."

Phillipus checked the urge to respond. The girl was vital to the future of the faith in Glenmara, but the idea of dying for Moloch had become singularly unappealing. If Moloch was so powerful, why was everything falling apart? The thought made him feel small and insecure. Though his mind raced with schemes, he was too frightened to do anything but follow instructions.

When Eowulf again laid eyes upon Aine his breath caught in his chest, and his fierce demeanor ebbed away. She remained flawless, the only thing on earth in the least worthwhile. "Biscuit," he said as though it were a prayer.

She went to him. Though she was aware that beneath that thin veneer of affection lurked the terror of a madman, his eyes were gentle and reassuring. "What are you doing?" she asked.

Trembling, he took her hand. "Sweet Biscuit! I came for you. The priest brought me, and now we're leaving. Isn't that right, priest?"

Phillipus nodded.

The fear in his eyes filled Aine with a perverse pleasure. "False priest!" she hissed. "Where is your god now?"

Eowulf pulled Aine close. "I came for you," he said.

She smiled. "To keep your promise, brave Eowulf. My champion," she said with real affection, though she knew that leaving with him was as dangerous as staying.

"Now show us the way out!" Eowulf ordered, and Phillipus led them through the pyramid.

They didn't get far. The alarm was instantly raised, and soon the temple was swarming with pursuers. Backed into a narrow alcove, Eowulf prepared to make his stand.

"There's no way out, Biscuit," he complained like a little boy. He looked for blame in Aine's eyes, but found them closed. Lost in the stronghold of the enemy, she had turned to God.

Eowulf braced himself in the doorway. "Come closer you pack of mangy ditch dogs!" he dared.

But instead the priests stopped, exchanged frightened whispers and cast anxious glances over their shoulders.

"The Legion," someone said. "The Legion has come."

"What? Where? Are you certain?"

"Yes! Out on the ridge! The Legion!"

"Why would they come here?"

"You fool! It's the girl. They've come for the girl!"

The mumbling became an anxious susurrus of fear.

"He shouldn't have brought her here."

"He's gone too far now!"

"Shut up! You're talking about the High Priest. You'll be on the altar next!"

"Soon there will be no altar! Didn't you hear? The Legion is out there."

"We have troops too!"

"The Legion is here! The Legion!"

"And they'll have done for the lot of you!" threatened Eowulf. He stepped out of the alcove, his merciless eyes promising ruin and death.

"The Legion!" cried someone, and hesitation became retreat. If the Legion had come to rescue the girl, they weren't going to risk harming her. In moments the hallway was empty.

"The Legion, eh?" chuckled Eowulf. "There's luck."

"Luck has nothing to do with it," Aine countered. "I prayed. God answered."

"You prayed for the Legion?"

"No, I just prayed. God picked the Legion."

Eowulf spat and growled. "Nonsense!"

Aine's eyes narrowed. "Think what you will. This isn't coincidence."

Eowulf gaped at the empty corridor. The Legion? It *was* difficult to believe. Yet everything that had already happened was beyond believing; Anwend Halfdane at the gate, Evan MacKeth in the chapel, and the unexplainable salvation they had just experienced. Coincidence? How was it possible?

"We're not delivered yet," Eowulf cautioned. "Lead us out, priest."

Phillipus did as he was told. Surviving was the only thing that seemed worthwhile, and with Eowulf's sword at his back even that seemed unlikely. He led them out into the chaos of the temple courtyard.

Priests and acolytes milled about with little discernible purpose. A cadre of well-trained temple soldiers formed up in the main yard, but no one appeared to be in charge.

At the stables, Eowulf and Aine secured horses and led them through the confused tangle of humanity to the north wall, where a small postern gate stood open. Mounting, Eowulf turned to Phillipus.

"Treacherous swine!" he snarled and made to strike the priest down.

As Phillipus closed his eyes in preparation for the end of his life, a prayer burst silently from the shadows of his twisted spirit. A supplication without form or direction, he hurled it blindly into unfamiliar realms, searching for the power of a God he had always denied. Somewhere the One True God reigned. But would such a God listen to his cry?

Eowulf's sword never fell. Aine Ceallaigh pulled at his arm. The voice of Claranides rose above the tumult of the crowd.

"Stop them! She is a gift to the god!"

Aine spurred her mount toward the gate as a sudden swarm of people pulled Eowulf from the saddle. He flailed at them, but there were too many, and they clawed him down. Then the girl charged back into the fray, her horse knocking people aside and trampling them under foot. She pulled Eowulf onto her own steed, and they charged through the gate to safety.

Eowulf's abandoned horse nudged Phillipus and slapped at the earth with one hoof. She snorted and tossed her head. An impossible thought lurched into the priest's mind. In an instant he was in the saddle, thundering toward the silent fastness of the Balinora Mountains.

——— ———

The messenger, having managed to sneak through the encampment on the plain, didn't get far once he entered Durham. He was beaten, interrogated and hanged in short order. The document he carried was brought to the Duke.

Fitzwarren had chosen an elegant residence in the upper town as his headquarters, but the opulence of his surroundings was having little effect on the success of his plans. Everything had ground to a frustrating halt.

"Look at this," Fitzwarren laughed, shoving the paper across the table to Broderick Laighan.

"What is it?"

"Read it."

Laighan took a moment to peruse the document. "Goblins have taken Gwenferew and overrun the countryside? Where did you get this?"

"A messenger from Morleigh Dunroon's manor. It's signed by his father."

"Well, if you can believe it, now we have a goblin problem," Laighan said.

"No. Dunroon's father has a goblin problem. Gwenferew has a goblin problem. Our problem is Osric Murchadha. Until we solve our problem, nothing else matters." He threw the letter onto a pile of other papers and went back to his meal.

CHAPTER V
CONVERGENCE

The ship took three agonizing days to reach Faltigern, tacking back and forth across the lake fighting contrary winds. Though he was so seasick that it was difficult to concentrate on anything else, Evan couldn't block out the deeper misery that stemmed from the loss of Aine and the disappearance of his Watcher.

Regardless of what happened at Moloch's temple, whether Aine was rescued or not, Evan knew he had lost her. Having abandoned her, how could he ever face her again? Surely she would understand he was only obeying God, wouldn't she? That's what he was doing, wasn't it? The vision yet lingered in his mind, but did that mean it came from God? There were other voices that could plague the minds of men. The Shadow Lord whispered from the darkness of Sheol, cajoling, tempting, offering sweet lies to confuse and misdirect. Wasn't it possible the vision came from that quarter?

Except it wasn't possible. For the hundredth time he reasoned it out, and for the hundredth time he knew he was doing the right thing. Not the desire of his heart, but the right thing.

In Faltigern, Evan lost no time securing a horse and other necessities for his journey. Right or wrong, true or false, the vision continued to grow more urgent and specific. A name thrust itself into his mind. He made inquiries.

"Oh that!" said the little man who sold maps in a small corner shop. "I knows that name, and I'll tell ya what I knows fer but three Krons."

Evan produced the coins.

"Clon Miarth: that's what they calls the meadows around Gwenferew. They stretch from the river all the way to the loch." He traced a route on a worn map with his crooked, ink stained finger. "Best cross the river at the Legion Bridge."

With growing despair, Evan turned north toward a meeting with the Red Goblin, Klabaga, in the bloody meadows of Clon Miarth.

——— ——— ———

Tribune Galba built his camp on the ridgeline above the Hinnom Valley. In view of the Great Temple, the legionaries dug a ditch, piled the spoil into a parapet, and constructed a palisade with rope and sharpened wooden stakes. At the end of every march into hostile territory, the Legion built a defensible camp and today they made a great show of their work, for an attentive audience watched their every move.

Across the valley a frenzy of activity began the moment the Legion appeared on the ridge. The afternoon sun glinted on spear points and helmets as men rushed into formation.

The Tribune watched the mercenaries across the valley grow more nervous by the moment. Recruited from the dark alleys of cities across Glenmara, they were bandits and murderers, thieves and varlets of the worst kind. Some were Legion deserters who weren't the least pleased at the arrival of their former comrades.

Formations began to dissolve before they could fully muster. Men slipped away in the confusion. One group seized horses and a pitched battle ensued. Confusion and dismay spread through the enemy camp and ended only after much of the place had gone up in flames.

Galba smiled and gave Brian a friendly wink.

"We've made them nervous."

Once the Legion completed its work, Galba fed and rested his men and then led a delegation under a flag of truce toward the temple. Halfway across the valley they were met by a small group of priests and soldiers.

"Hail!" the Tribune said cheerfully, "I am Tribune Lucius Galba."

"What are you doing here Tribune?" demanded the senior priest, "The Legion has no business in this valley."

"I beg to differ. The king of Glenmara sent me to retrieve a stolen treasure. Unless it is returned, there will be bloodshed."

"You dare threaten us?" the priest blustered. "Everything within the Temple walls belongs to the God, not the king. If you make a move toward us you'll be slaughtered."

"By whom? This rabble you've raised? The assassins you've got behind those walls? Deliver the living person of Aine Ceallaigh into my hands or I will come and take her."

"You don't dare . . ."

"Of course I do. Further, I assure you that if we meet resistance of any sort, if one of my legionaries even stumbles on a stone as we march up the hill, I'll burn your temple to the ground. I give you one hour, priest. Not much time."

The temple delegation hurried away and Lucius Galba returned to his encampment. Before the hour was up, he set his command marching toward the temple in two tight columns five ranks deep. Cavalry covered either flank, and a small knot of archers followed behind.

In spite of their superior numbers the enemy didn't dare meet the Legion in the open valley, so they threw up barricades along the steep slope of the ridge and blocked the narrow roadway with stones and tables and wagons and whatever came to hand. Galba was disappointed that his opponents wouldn't come out to play, but he hadn't really expected they would. The reputation of the Legion had already accomplished a great deal. Now Legion steel would do the rest. He nodded to his Centurion, Corwyn Donnachadh, and set his plan in motion.

At the base of the slope where the road zigzagged up toward the temple, the Legion formation shifted from column into line in a perfectly executed maneuver. Without pause they continued up the ridge.

The enemy had set its defensive line halfway up the hill where the road turned a third time. For the duration of their ascent the legionaries would be under missile fire, and soon arrows and spears began to rain down among them.

"Form testudo!" thundered Galba.

"Testudo!" roared the Centurion.

The line altered step. Equipment shifted with silent precision and within seconds every legionary was covered front, flank and overhead by a flexible armored shell of overlapping shields. To the defenders it appeared that the Legion had been transformed into a gigantic creature with bright red scales, shuffling toward them on hundreds of legs.

The resolve of the remaining mercenaries began to waver. Though they still outnumbered the advancing legionaries, each man waiting behind the barricades silently calculated the amount of his pay against the value he placed on his life. The mathematics couldn't be reconciled. Legion arrows hissed down into their ranks. Men fell screaming.

"Spears!" ordered the Tribune.

"Spears!" crowed the Centurion and the testudo dissolved as quickly as it had appeared. "Now!"

Half a hundred iron tipped shafts arched up from the second rank and impacted on the mercenary line. Shields were pierced, men impaled. The cloying smell of blood wafted unpleasantly on the afternoon breeze. Before the first volley had been absorbed, another followed and a third, and the

Border Legion pushed over the barricade into the staggered ranks of their opponents.

The line broke, scattering back toward the temple compound. Officers mustered other formations in the narrow field before the gateway, but what tenuous control they held over their troops evaporated when the compound gate was slammed shut in their faces. The priests were abandoning them! What was left of the line collapsed, scattering men in all directions.

Galba sent his cavalry in pursuit of the disordered enemy, dressed his lines and turned his attention to the gate.

"Send them up," he ordered Corwyn.

"Optio Brannon!" cried the Centurion, "Deploy your squad!"

Ropes and grapples arched into the air, followed by legionaries who scrambled to the top of the undefended wall. Within moments the gates swung open, and Galba led his men into the temple compound.

They made directly for the black stone pyramid where several hundred armed men had gathered on the central platform.

"Assassins," the Tribune confided to Brian. "They're good at killing, but they're terrible soldiers."

As if in response to the insult, the entire tangled group rushed down the stairs and impacted on the Legion line in a startling crash of bodies and weapons. Screams and curses punctuated the air. Men fell and were trampled beneath the inexorable advance of the superbly trained legionaries.

But though untrained in fighting as a unit, the zeal of the Assassins to defend their sacred ground was such that Legion blood too stained the ground before the temple.

In the end Moloch's men couldn't prevent their enemies from pushing up the pyramid steps. They fled to the massive bronze doors, turned for a final stand and were overwhelmed in a burst of violence that not only ended all resistance, but secured entry to the interior as well.

"Corwyn," said Galba as he cleaned his sword on the cloak of a dead Assassin, "I want this compound under control before we set foot inside the temple."

"Domini!" returned the Centurion and dispatched his men to all corners of the yard. Once satisfied with Corwyn's efforts, Galba led a reinforced Century into the pyramid.

Inside, resistance was minimal. The remaining priests were anxious to escape and hindered the Legion only by their frenzied presence. The few that intentionally got in the way were dealt with quickly and severely. In short order the legionaries arrived at the Chamber of Sacrifice.

Brian charged into the circular enclosure ahead of the others. Across the room Claranides waited while several clerics dragged a struggling, blond-haired girl toward a white marble altar.

"No!" Brian bellowed, took a single step and was beset by a dozen men who leapt from the shadows with swords and daggers. Had legionaries not come to his aide he might have perished, for as it was, the fight in that dark, evil place was merciless and brutal, leaving the floor tangled with the dead from both sides.

The rescued girl flung herself screaming into Brian's arms, but she was not Aine Ceallaigh. At the altar Claranides cried out for a destroyer to scour the world of the One True God and His followers. His answer was the eerie mocking echo of wounded and dying men.

Galba pushed the High Priest against the wall with the tip of his sword. "Where is Aine Ceallaigh?"

Claranides hesitated, and Brian seized him by the throat. "Aine Ceallaigh or I'll break your neck! Where is she?"

The High Priest stared past Brian to the carnage at his feet. At every hand, reminders of failure taunted him - the presence of the Legion, the girl he had chosen to sacrifice after Aine Ceallaigh's escape, the dead priests scattered about the floor. A freezing fear crawled through his blood, an unfamiliar sensation to the man whose power in Glenmara had once been absolute. But all that changed once Osric Murchadha fell beneath the spell of Iosa Christus. Everything had begun to unravel after that - the edicts outlawing human sacrifice, the banishment of the priesthood and now the temple violated, Moloch's faithful dead, captured or scattered.

Brian redoubled his grip on the prisoner. "Answer me, curse your black heart!"

"This man will kill you if you don't answer," interjected Galba. "Be quick! Where is the girl?"

"Get out! Get out do you hear? You've brought sacrilege to this temple!"

"The girl, vermin, or I'll gut you like a fish!"

Claranides shook his head. "There is no girl!"

Before Brian could kill him, Galba and several legionaries wrestled the priest to the floor.

"If she's here, we'll find her," assured the Tribune.

They searched but didn't find Aine. The moon was well up by the time the Legion retired to their encampment, carrying with them their dead, wounded and more than fifty prisoners. In the desperate darkness of that warm spring night Brian Beollan continued to search the temple. In the morning Galba found him sitting atop the temple steps weeping like a child.

———————

Padraigh's scouts found the enemy deployed in a tight circle around Durham. The Dragon Man's ferry was heavily guarded, and patrols secured all the roads. But one approach remained open.

Below the falls near the town of Doone, a seldom-used ford remained unguarded. In the best circumstances it provided a treacherous crossing, but Padraigh had to get his troops across the river where they could approach Durham through good open country from the south. With the main of the enemy staged between the two rivers south of the town, he might pin them against the city and break the siege. To accomplish this feat he had mustered a force of four hundred cavalry and twelve hundred infantry, including the Provisional Militia from Faltigern.

Throughout the long, miserable night, the little army clawed its way across the swollen river, and before sunrise the crossing was complete. Still, before they turned toward Durham, the river had claimed a score of good men.

In the early morning of the following day Padraigh drew his men up onto the field before Durham. Behind hastily constructed earthworks, a great encampment spread across the meadows below the outer town. Cooking fires cast smoke skyward, and the aroma of breakfast reminded Padraigh's exhausted men of their own hunger. But there would be no food for any of them short of capturing the enemy camp.

Padraigh deployed his infantry in two ranks, four files deep. Behind these a paltry reserve brought up the rear while the cavalry screened either flank. As first light touched the eastern horizon they advanced on the city.

The enemy had anchored its defensive line on a small stone tower that guarded the crossroads south of the town. To neutralize the threat of the tower, Padraigh shifted his cavalry to the right flank and hinged his left against the River Gabhailin. In this manner he planned to force his way through the right of the enemy line.

They advanced without fanfare accompanied by the ubiquitous jingle of armor, the creaking of leather and the heavy tread of man and horse upon the dew moistened ground. Trumpets sounded in the enemy camp, and troops rushed onto the plain to form larger units. Padraigh's army slammed against the earthworks near the river.

From the top of the keep, high above the Sceir Naid, Martin watched as the advancing line lapped against the earthworks and then began to bend and break up. From such distance he could hear very little, the repetitive notes of trumpets and the faint clatter and clash of far away battle. The ant-like figures hardly seemed real, the event unconnected to what was happening at the palace. But the boy knew that men were dying down there, and that the outcome of that distant struggle would decide the fate of everyone involved in this terrible business. Someone had come to save them--Padraigh or Brian or perhaps even his master. Whoever it was they were badly outnumbered. Then Martin saw soldiers gathering in the palace yard and hurried down to join them.

Enemy forces poured from the town to meet the threat. Cavalry wheeled out in a long arch and smashed headlong into the screen of horsemen guarding the right of the infantry advance. A desperate fight raged for control of the river fortifications.

Padraigh bullied, threatened, and hit at his men with the flat of his sword. Untrained as an army, exhausted, hungry and thrust into combat against better-trained and better-equipped troops, it was pointless to expect much from them. Their own commanders were doing their utmost to urge them on to greater effort, and still it wasn't enough.

Punctuated by a blasphemous curse, Padraigh committed his reserves, though he knew in doing so he had lost the battle. Even if they managed to break the line, the enemy was mustering fresh troops who would soon join the battle. But there was no use holding anything back.

With the added weight of reinforcements they breached the earthworks and pushed out toward the lower town. Here, drawn up in ordered ranks, Duke Fitzwarren's army awaited them. The militia tried to reform their lines.

Padraigh's men were nearly spent, and the battle had only begun. Now faced with the daunting spectacle of the enemy's superior numbers arrayed across the field, fear was becoming as tangible to them as the army they faced. If they didn't rally now they would break before another blow could be struck.

"Your king is up there!" Padraigh yelled, pointing to the Sceir Naid standing like a stone giant above the countryside. "He's watching you from his high place. Will you shame yourselves? What will men say of you tomorrow? Will they speak of your courage or will they laugh and shake their heads because you were found wanting?"

Their faces betrayed a confusion of responses. Some were ready to attack on the instant. Some couldn't even hear what Padraigh was saying. Most were carefully considering the best way to stay alive. If they fell apart they would be hunted down piecemeal, but if they stayed? Commanders and officers barked orders and pulled men into line. The enemy moved toward them in steel covered ranks, weapons glistening in the fierce light of early morning.

Roused from his bed at the first trumpet call, Duke Robert Fitzwarren was alarmed to find a hostile army at his back. He cursed the delays that had beset his efforts, leading to this latest unfortunate turn of events. Yet observing the small force opposing him, his apprehension faded. He didn't know who was attacking his camp but he intended to crush them for their arrogance.

Arrows arched into the mass of Padraigh's infantry causing casualties and increasing the uncertainty of the troops. They huddled behind their shields unwilling to go forward, waiting for the first man to turn and run so that they might follow without shame.

In the midst of his admonishment, an arrow burst through Padraigh's mailed shoulder. Those nearby saw him reach up, break off the head of the missile and withdraw the shaft as though it wasn't imbedded in his flesh. He flung the bloody tip to the ground, turned, and roaring like a wild thing, charged the approaching enemy.

Incredulous, the militiamen exchanged glances. An officer picked up the discarded arrowhead and tucked it safely in his belt.

"Come on then!" he shouted and inspired beyond their fear they rushed forward.

Osric knew this unexpected attack was his only chance to break the siege. With so many troops being withdrawn from the town to meet the new threat, it was time for those in the Sceir Naid to do their part. Leaving a small detachment behind, the king led his followers into the town.

There was little resistance at first. The unexpected appearance of Padraigh's army had practically stripped the town bare. But as they approached the gate between the upper and lower town, they were met with a violent swarm of heavily armed soldiers.

The two masses collided with a great cry and the lines of struggling men began to spread left and right. Those coming from behind pushed at their fellows, producing a writhing tangle of men hemmed together by the pressure of their movement and the houses and buildings surrounding them. Men fell wounded and dead to further entangle the remaining combatants.

Reinforcements arrived, threatening to envelope Osric's force on two sides. Dunroon and his men were pushed back, their lines buckling, and it might have ended badly without the appearance of Anwend Halfdane and his wild-eyed Varangians on the right flank.

The battle shifted. Fitzwarren's men began to break, and with one more push their line dissolved into complete chaos. The besiegers fled in all directions, throwing aside weapons in their mad haste to escape. In earnest pursuit Osric's men cut them down, burst into the lower town and charged toward the battle on the plain.

Fed by hunger, exhaustion and the pain from his broken leg, Padraigh's anger was already intense. It grew more reckless still as he saw his attempt to rescue the king fall apart before his eyes. Then some upstart of a peasant archer shot a clothyard shaft through his shoulder.

Breaking off the protruding shaft had nearly caused him to swoon, but the pain had also focused his rage. Someone was going to pay for everything he had been through over the past week, and with that wild, irrational thought he charged toward the advancing army.

Arrows hissed through the crisp morning air like deadly raindrops of steel. Some glanced from his armor or thudded into his shield, but Padraigh urged his horse on. *Just let me lay steel to these impudent fellows!* he thought. Then his horse screamed, stumbled and fell, an arrow sunk to the fletching in its straining flank.

In a cloud of dust, amid the flailing limbs of his dying steed, Padraigh came down like a stone. In the eruption of pain that followed, his anger reached such a peak that had he been killed in that instant, he might not have noticed. Before he came to a jolting stop he tried to regain his feet.

"Now they've done for my horse!" he spit between broken teeth.

He rose screaming invective, spouting blood in a crimson spray from battered lips. His shield hung from a useless arm. Sword gone, he reached for his dagger and tried to advance the few yards separating him from his foes. His broken leg collapsed, and he fell, only to rise as the enemy line advanced. Before it could reach him, Padraigh's own infantry arrived.

"Padraigh to the rear!" someone yelled and gently, insistently and despite his fierce protests, they moved him out of harm's way. An instant later the Faltigern Militia closed with Duke Fitzwarren's army. Wild, desperate combat erupted across the plain.

Fitzwarren shifted troops to reinforce his right flank. It wouldn't take much to push his opponents into the river. He glanced back at the frowning mass of the Sceir Naid and hoped that Osric was watching. Perhaps in a few hours the king would be more amenable to terms.

More men came out of the town. Even now a large group spilled out onto what had been the fairgrounds just a few days before. With those and the men from the left flank he would put a quick end to the opposing force.

The renewed enthusiasm of the militia had already been ground into uselessness by the grist of exhaustion and superior numbers. Casualties, though light thus far, would blossom into wholesale slaughter once the line broke or was pushed into the river. The narrowest margin separated whether it was better to die fighting or perish attempting to escape.

Fitzwarren waved impatiently at the men coming from the town. Once they arrived he would send them to envelope Padraigh's infantry, but as they drew closer, a chill of fear overcame him.

"Osric!" he cursed.

Before he had fully formed the words the King's men reached the rear of his formation. With a roar that seemed to shake the very air they threw themselves into the fray.

They were only a handful. By comparison to the numbers they faced, their appearance on the field might have made no difference to the outcome of the battle had they not burst so unexpectedly upon the rear of Duke Fitzwarren's struggling infantry, scattered the archers and rolled up the enemy's flank.

Fitzwarren cursed and called for his reserves. If they came quickly he might yet salvage the moment. But seeing the sudden change of fortune visited upon their fellows, they hesitated, and in doing so victory became bitter defeat. Those who moments before had been on the verge of breaking Padraigh's army now abandoned their weapons and fled the field.

They made for the town. Yet there was no safety in that quarter. Before they had gotten any distance at all Anwend Halfdane and his Varangians cut them off.

None of the participants fully understood what was happening. Neither the men of Padraigh nor of the King nor of Duke Fitzwarren knew anything save the events occurring in the few feet surrounding them, though all were part of the chaos and fear and elation of the greater battle. Least of all did young Martin Reamon understand what was transpiring.

He had followed the king into the streets without time to contemplate what he was doing.

The fight at the gate to the lower town was sudden and confused. From the back of the column he had been part of the general press but saw no fighting himself. Then the charge out onto the plain where he found himself thrust amongst the Varangians, and even in the midst of these wild warriors who fought with such abandon, he found no employment for the sword he had taken from the dead legionary. He was helplessly borne along in the wake of their savagery.

As the fight degenerated into pursuit, the remainder of Fitzwarren's troops broke. They still possessed the numbers to reverse their defeat, indeed, the slaughter of Padraigh's cavalry continued, but they had lost heart and wouldn't respond to orders.

Robert Fitzwarren watched his dreams of kingship vanish. He fumbled with the reins of his horse and thought it a bitter irony that *rein* should sound so much like *reign* and still miss the mark entirely. There would be no reign for him now, no reward for all his efforts. He drew his sword.

Broderick Laighan galloped up, eyes wild, sweat streaming from his face despite the cool air of morning.

"What are you doing? If we can rally . . ."

"Rally? Don't you see what's happened? They've beaten us!"

He pointed at the soldiers fleeing south. Many of them hadn't struck a blow. Laighan, seeing that Fitzwarren wasn't going to listen, ordered the trumpeter to recall the cavalry, but intent on exploiting their success, they didn't respond.

Laighan clutched at Fitzwarren's arm. "It's time to go," he warned, but his companion shrugged away his hand. There was one remaining option that would expiate the failure of his plans and the utter ruin of his ambitions. If he couldn't be king, neither would Osric.

He spurred his mount into the tide of men, laying about with his sword. Hands grabbed at him, blades glanced from his armor until he was pulled from his horse screaming and cursing Osric's name. His corpse was discovered at sunset, his dreams vanished into the dust.

The battle degenerated into a chase where the greatest slaughter occurred. Yet the carnage didn't last long. Padraigh's troops were incapable of serious pursuit, and there were still organized enemy units just beyond the river Cuinn.

The victors suffered remarkably light casualties: fifty dead and twice as many of Padraigh's infantry wounded. His cavalry was another matter. Although throughout the day, the remains of Ferghal's horsemen straggled back into town, few had survived. In contrast, more than six hundred enemy dead wove a carpet of mangled bodies across the plain. Roughly half that number had been taken prisoner with more being added by the hour.

Sporadic fighting continued as small pockets of resistance were overcome in the town, but by the end of the day Durham was secure. The remaining enemy dispersed. Broderick Laighan gathered what forces he could and withdrew to his holdings in the west. The siege was over.

The following morning Osric was presented with the documents and correspondence taken from Robert Fitzwarren's headquarters. Here he discovered the letter from Morleigh Dunroon's father.

By the time Osric had read the message his hands were trembling. The dispatch from Giomer Lorich, the finger, the horrible creature they had fished from the river and this. Now there was no doubt what was happening in Gwenferew. Everything was coming together in a horrible mosaic that promised to prolong the bloodshed and misery far beyond what they had already suffered. Poor Evan's prophetic vision of impending doom had been more accurate than even he might have dreamed, and that dream was now grown to nightmare proportions.

Osric looked out across the recent field of battle. Parties had begun the grisly task of burying the dead whose bodies were already providing the kites and vultures a gruesome banquet. How many more had perished in Gwenferew? How many more would lay cold and quiet beneath the sky before this horrible business was done? As far as he could see and in whichever direction he looked there was nothing but war. The first battle was won, but Duke Laighan had escaped with a large part of his forces intact. Osric would have to deal with him sooner or later, and the longer that reckoning was postponed the deadlier the encounter would be. And now there was Gwenferew, the whisper of a brutal future; goblins come to the world of men.

Long before he called for his commanders Osric decided to turn north, north toward Gwen-ferew and the first battle of what he feared would become a long and bloody war.

———————

Going back for Eowulf was one of the worst decisions Aine ever made, and she bitterly regretted it now. Yet when she saw him pulled from his horse in the temple yard she acted out of instinct. Kidnapper or not, he had rescued her.

However faulty her logic might have been, there was no reversing her decision now as they galloped toward Loch Aiden. But though Aine had hoped to find her way to safety with the Border Legion, they hadn't gone a mile when they discovered a large body of horsemen converging on them. Though still distant, it was plain they weren't riding Legion horses. As she turned her mount north, Aine's safety slipped rapidly away.

On and on in a mind numbing progression of miserable hours that broadened into miserable days, they pushed their steed to the brink of collapse. Broken by stolen moments of restless sleep, their journey took them ever north along the rugged coast of Loch Aiden. At a small fishing village where the river swept out into the loch, they turned west, and Eowulf forced passage across the Aiden on a small ferry.

They had almost reached the far shore when their pursuers entered the village behind them. Until this moment Eowulf had been blindly running, as if he might escape his disastrous life by speed and distance covered. Now he cast desperately about for a refuge, a place to hide until he could find a way to salvage whatever was left of the future. He couldn't go home. None of the major towns would be safe. In the end he determined there was but one place where he might find a measure of safety: Dhub.

A mining town until the silver ran out, Dhub was a refuge for outlaws and undesirables. There among the outcasts he could rest and come up with another plan. It was a long way, but there were no other options.

Others had run out of options too. Riding north along the lakeshore, recently escaped from the catastrophic events at Moloch's temple, Bran Mael Morda considered his next move. With him rode sixteen men who had followed him since they deserted from the Second Glenmaran Border Legion two years before. Now they followed him into an ever-tightening circle that was likely to end in their capture and execution. Desertion from the Legion meant death.

His career as a bandit along the southern trade routes had been profitable until an unfortunate encounter with a book merchant and a young bowman. Bran fidgeted in the saddle at the remembrance of that debacle. Three of his men had been killed that day and seven crippled before they captured the mischievous marksman. That should have been the end of the young fool, but instead they let him go. Not only that, they carried him, badly wounded, to an orphanage in Glenne. He still didn't quite understand why.

It had proved their undoing. Shortly after leaving Glenne they were ambushed by the local militia, and although they fought their way out, all the wounded in his band were captured and two others killed. The survivors were pursued for several days during which time yet another of their number was killed in an accident with his horse. At length they found themselves in the service of Moloch, recruited to protect the Great Temple. A worthwhile idea at the time, with the appearance of the Legion Bran decided to move on.

Now they were bound for Dhub. Durham was out of the question, Faltigern and Gwenferew untenable, and the High Priest had his own problems. Dhub would have to do until he could come up with something better.

He growled quietly. Everything had unraveled after that bowman. He suspected the boy's god was displeased that his servant had been injured; the wounds Dungal inflicted on him doubtlessly proved fatal. Now Iosa Christus was angry and Bran was running for his life.

Someone else was making haste on the trail ahead of Bran's company. Two people on a single horse, he had seen them once or twice in the distance. Now as they approached the village at the head of the lake, he saw them again as they scrambled up the far riverbank and made away in a cloud of dust. He wondered if they too were refugees from the temple, running from the justice of the Legion or the wrath of the One True God.

———————

Much to the dismay of everyone, Little Wren arrived in the Legion fortress none the worse for his trip, albeit imparted with a singular stench from the gutter. Taken to Tribune Ronan he delivered his report.

Ronan had groomed himself for command, and now with Giomer locked in his rooms, it was the perfect opportunity to take charge. But loyalty demanded he make a final attempt to rescue his commander's honor. The men were already starting to grumble. The official word was that Giomer had taken ill, but that wouldn't wash for long. Ronan headed for Giomer's house.

As he approached, it became apparent that something irregular was going on in the guardroom. A large knot of legionaries milled about the doorway. There was shouting.

Ronan shoved his way into the small trophy room where he was met with a remarkable sight. An entire squad of slightly battered legionaries struggled to hold Braslav Tlapinski against the wall. The room was in shambles, with tables upset and captured flags and war trophies scattered about the floor among shards of wood from splintered furniture.

"What's all this?" demanded the Tribune.

Braslav pushed away from the wall bellowing an incomprehensible explanation, and only by a supreme effort were the legionaries able to push him back again.

"He wanted to see the commander and wouldn't take no for an answer."

"That's right sir," complained another, slurring words through a bloody lip, "and when we tried to send him away he went mad!"

"That's enough!" ordered Ronan. "Calm yourself Father, or I'll have you clapped in irons!"

Braslav nodded, but the wild excitement in his eyes remained.

"Now what do you mean by this? Are you drunk or have you truly gone mad?"

"Oh, he's been drinking all right," quipped a legionary.

"Silence!" roared the Tribune. "I'll have order if I have to flog every man in this room!"

At that moment the adjacent door crashed open, and amid a descending dread, Giomer staggered into the room. It appeared he had been dragged behind a horse. His clothing was disheveled and dirty, his hair matted and mussed, his beard untrimmed and unkept. Bloodshot, uncomprehending eyes darted about the room searching for something relevant in his surroundings. He leaned against the doorframe as though he couldn't trust his own legs.

"Commander Lorich," said Ronan and started toward him.

Giomer raised his hand and shook his head. He knew he must look a sight. His nerves had been jolted by the screams of the wretched people the goblins had tortured to death, but he knew his duty, knew what he owed the men in his command. The thumping and yelling had roused him and now he had to respond.

"What sort of mischief have we here?" he asked in a painful, forced whisper.

Everyone tried to answer at once, and Giomer had to call for silence to get an explanation that made sense. "Well," he said advancing on Braslav, "what have you to say?"

Braslav blinked. The strange bird had told him many things about Iosa Christus and the dark spirit that hovered over Gwenferew. But how to explain them? He didn't understand much of it himself. Still, unless he could convince these men they would all die.

He blurted out, "I know how to save the town!"

Giomer's eyes gleamed without mirth. "Indeed? Well, I've never rejected a good idea. What wisdom have you that will save the day?"

Braslav hesitated. How could he tell these men anything? They were the finest soldiers in the world. Yet his solution had nothing to do with strategy or tactics or skill with weapons. It was something more powerful that any of those things.

"We've got to pray," he said timidly, his resolve wavering under the scrutiny of so many mighty men of war. "If we pray we'll see the better side of this."

Giomer came further into the room. His gait remained unsteady, but his face was remarkably animated. "What did you say?" he asked.

"We must pray," replied Braslav.

Giomer smelled the odor of cheap wine on Braslav's breath. "And to whom must we pray, little father?"

"Why Iosa Christus, of course."

Giomer shook his head and sighed. "To think I missed that! All my training and experience, and yet you're the one who brings me this revelation. How did you uncover this secret?"

Braslav spoke before he thought. "A little bird told me . . ."

The explosion that followed surprised everyone, especially the unfortunate Braslav, for he found himself on the floor with Giomer astride his chest.

"The world is falling apart and you're talking to little birds? Get this idiot out of here! Put him in the gaol, d'ya hear? Have him executed! I'll carry out the sentence myself!"

He seized a sword from a nearby sentry, and the legionaries, not wishing Braslav to come to real harm, quickly dragged the unhappy man away. Giomer stormed about the room yelling and brandishing the weapon for a few moments while Tribune Ronan looked on.

"The nerve of that fool!" he exclaimed. "Barging in here with such nonsense! A little bird indeed!"

Then, much to Ronan's relief, the commander of the Legion in Gwenferew sat down on the floor and laughed until tears streamed down his unshaven face. A little bird indeed!

———

In the dark confines of the Legion jail, Braslav Tlapinski wept at his own stupidity. Why had he listened to that bird? Why had he mentioned any of it to Giomer? Of course they thought him drunk or mad! That bird! Where was the cursed thing now?

"I'm right here," said a horribly familiar voice from the shadows of the cell.

Braslav shook his fist. "Go away! You've ruined whatever reputation I had with those lads. These people don't believe in Iosa Christus, and they didn't like the prayer idea at all!"

"Humans are like that," said Julian sadly. "Admit it. You don't like the prayer idea either, do you? Nobody does. Humans are determined to take control when the real answer is to be still and know that Iosa is God."

"What do you know about it?" raged Braslav. "Have you seen those creatures out there? How can we sit back and do nothing? They'll have us for lunch!"

The bird hopped closer and made a funny noise. "You don't understand any of this. Nobody suggested doing nothing, but you cannot fight this spirit with steel! Pray, foolish man, and take God's message to those around you."

"How can I do that now? I'm in jail! I knew this would happen!"

"What a spectacle you make of yourself. Just pray and trust that God will answer. Wait, watch and worship. The answers will come."

With that the strange bird vanished as quickly as he had come, leaving Braslav alone in the dark again. He was unhappy and tired, but he prayed just in case the bird was right.

———————

While the improbable exchange between Julian and Braslav took place, Giomer Lorich listened to Legionary Wren's report. For a moment he dwelt upon the humorous irony that much like Braslav, a little bird was speaking to him. He smiled at the absurdity.

Giomer sent Wren back into the drainage ditch with a Legion signal horn strapped to his back and then summoned his officers. In the morning, if the town hall still held, they would attempt a rescue.

———————

The sun would be up soon. The discomfort crept upon Klabaga as the eastern horizon displayed the first gleamings of the new day. Though he was accustomed to it by now, it remained a source of constant irritation. But something besides the sun was making his hackles rise.

The Red Goblin climbed to the top of a tower and looked out over the dark meadows. Beyond sight and hearing, somewhere in the strange world of man, Evan MacKeth was coming to him. The young boy that had killed the Glamorth was coming to the corpse-strewn meadows of Clon Miarth, and here Klabaga would slay him. It was more than a matter of pride that the goblin desired his death. In the dark recesses of his spirit Klabaga knew that Evan MacKeth must perish, or he would never fulfill his destiny.

The rhythmic clack of gears and ratchets drew his attention to the courtyard where goblins worked at the mechanism of one of the three catapults brought from the mountain. They had been bombarding the town hall most of the night and were becoming quite accurate. A few hours earlier, part of the building collapsed under the weight of well-aimed stones, but the subsequent assault had been decisively repulsed.

The catapult bucked and released another heavy stone in a dull grey arch across the brightening sky. It came down with a crash accompanied by the sound of splintering timber and cracking mortar. Soon they would have done with the Town Hall.

He was about to descend the tower when the distant notes of a horn echoed through the still morning air. Nearby another took up the call, and before the sound died away the humans in the town hall poured out into the plaza. Klabaga hurried down to the street.

Goblins swarmed out of buildings to meet the new threat. Klabaga knew that the Legion fortress was stirring too, but he couldn't worry about that now. His job was to keep the men in the town hall from escaping.

Ugrik had already taken most of the army to pillage the countryside, leaving only enough warriors to keep the human-men in the city contained. The goblins still outnumbered the humans, but discipline wasn't what it might have been.

The goblins were still gathering as Tyrus led everyone down the central street. At the same moment, two centuries from the Legion fortress pushed south to occupy the goblins in the western plaza and east to link up with Tyrus. The Optio had arranged the militia in a tight wedge at the front of the column, filling the center with those who couldn't fight, the very young, the very old and the sick and wounded. The balance formed a rear guard. If everything worked properly most of them would be saved. If not . . . well, they would have died in the town hall anyway.

Once beyond the plaza, Tyrus placed the senior legionary in command, and with Angus and Wren, slipped into an alley. Carrying jars of oil, tinder and flint they hurried through the narrow, debris-strewn alleys, hiding from errant groups of goblins. As sounds of battle began to build in the west, they reached their goal.

Three heavy catapults stood side by side in a small courtyard. Constructed of heavy timber, banded in iron and tensioned with heavy lengths of twisted rope, they could throw an eighty-pound stone hundreds of yards. As the goblins had already proven, with these machines they could smash the human fortifications at their leisure.

Rushing through the broad courtyard gate the legionaries dispatched the startled goblin crews and immediately set to work. While Angus hammered at the metal gears, bending and breaking teeth, Tyrus and Wren soaked the wooden beams with oil and set them alight. Then they stood at the courtyard entrance and prepared to defend the place until the siege engines burned beyond repair.

The fight in the western plaza intensified. The century defending the southern approaches was engaged in a stiff fight against mounting odds, but the other century had already reached the column from the town hall. Detouring them to a carefully selected side street, the Legion ushered them behind and blocked the path with a phalanx of steel and crimson shields. Upon this the goblins angrily hurled themselves, but they could not stir the solid Legion ranks.

They withdrew in good order to the fortress and were soon safely inside. The operation had been flawlessly performed, and although the goblins immediately launched an attack on the compound, it was quickly repulsed.

Even Tyrus' foray succeeded. Before the goblins recognized what was happening, the siege machines were reduced to as many piles of charred beams and twisted metal. Yet the bravery and skill of the three intrepid legionaries wasn't enough to save themselves. Overwhelmed by a riot of furious goblins, the heroes fell fighting.

Along the highway to Gwenferew as it wound its way north through the rolling hills bordering Loch Aiden, Evan MacKeth rode toward Clon Miarth. There amidst the tall grasses he would find Klabaga and kill him. But to face Klabaga, he had given up Aine. The colors she had stitched for him were still tied to his arm, but he felt unworthy of them now. She had chosen him as her champion when he was too ill to take up arms, and now that he was whole again he had abandoned her. The farther he traveled from the Hinnom Valley, the more bitter and desperate his spirit became.

"Faith isn't what you feel," Julian once told him. *"Faith is claiming the mercy of the Christus even when your mortal flesh denies it."* So he rode, west and north, clinging to his Faith through the doubt.

He passed through a small village where peasants worked the fields beside a rustic manor house. It reminded him of his mother's fief in O'Byrne, his fief. Osric had given it to him. But Osric might already be dead, and the land now controlled by someone else. Not that the land mattered; he would have gladly traded every acre for Aine's sake.

Then one afternoon less than a day's ride from Gwenferew, Evan came upon something he hadn't seen in his vision. Rain had been falling since early morning and had long ago drenched him through, numbing his senses to the point that he wasn't even aware he was being watched or that anyone was interested in what he was doing. But he was very aware of the aroma of roasting meat, and soon the smell completely overpowered the odor of rain and mud and wet horse. It had been days since he had eaten a good meal.

Caution screamed in his ear. It might be anyone cooking a meal in the forest beside the river. It might be goblins in the cool shadow of the trees. It was better to stay in the open where his horse might give him some advantage. But that smell! At length he decided to reconnoiter.

"He's coming in," whispered a voice.

"Let 'im come then," growled another.

Evan hadn't gone a dozen paces into the trees when he was pulled from his horse and thrown violently into the mud. Before he could draw breath he found himself surrounded by three ragged men, one of who held a spear point against his chest.

"*Brilliant,*" thought Evan. "*Killed by a fondness for meat!*"

"What're ye doin skulking about?" asked the man with the spear.

"I'm hungry. I smelled food."

The man smirked. "Well, we ain't stole a cow so's you can eat, now did we lads?"

The others laughed.

"My mistake," apologized Evan with a shrug.

"Oh aye, that it were young 'un, a mistake you may never get over d'ya see?" warned one of the men.

"Shut yer gob fer a minute," said the man with the spear. "Look 'ere boy, ain't I know you?"

Evan didn't answer.

"Yeah, I've seen you somewhere, ain't it? What's yer name, little man?"

Evan didn't remember any of these men though he carefully studied their faces for any clue

152

that might stir his memory. He didn't dare reveal his true identity, so he gave them a name he had used before.

"Kevin Mac Maoilorian," he said.

The spearman's face broke into a craggy grin. "That's it! I knew I'd seen you! Dungal! Come see what I've caught!"

Dungal? The name brought a flood of unpleasant memories, but it wasn't until the man appeared that Evan realized the depth of his folly. Towering above him stood the bandit giant he had fought not a year past. Against all chance he had stumbled into Bran Mael Morda's band. "*Not again!*" he thought, the cold ice of fear coursing through his veins.

Dungal squinted, scratched his beard and then leapt into the air with a great roar. He shoved the spearman away and pulled the youth off the ground by a single massive hand clutched around the collar of Evan's shirt. "Bowman!" he cried, throwing both arms around the boy, "You're alive! Why didn't you die?"

"My God is merciful," Evan replied.

The words had a remarkable effect on Dungal. His exuberant, joyous demeanor instantly changed to one of reverence and awe. He released Evan and looked sheepishly down at him.

"Ya should've died from the wounds I gave ya, or been crippled and useless." He turned to the others. "You saw it, didn't ya? Who could have survived what I did to him, eh?" Dungal seemed almost proud of the wounds he had inflicted in that long ago, forlorn moment. "Yer God spared ya, didn't he bowman?"

Evan nodded. "Yes, He did."

"And you spared me. We might both have been bones by now cause of that fight, but here we are together standing in the rain! Did ya spare me 'cause of yer God, bowman?"

At the time Evan couldn't have said why he spared this giant, but he knew now that God had been directing him even then.

"Aye Dungal, God bid me spare you."

Dungal smiled wistfully, if such an expression were possible on such a face. His eyes glowed with pleasure as though Evan had shared a great secret with him. He nodded.

"Well good on you then," he enthused. "Come on bowman! Let's find Bran!"

Clapping a huge hand on Evan's shoulder he led him through the trees, past a line of tethered ponies and into a small encampment on the slopes of a gentle hill. Here, a dozen or more men squatted around a fire over which roasted the better part of a butchered cow. Evan hoped that whatever else occurred they would let him eat.

As they approached the fire Dungal called out. "Bran! Look what I've found. Ain't it queer?"

The grizzled, bearded face of Bran Mael Morda looked up. The mad flight from the temple and the lack of food and shelter had put him in a wretched mood, only partially improved by the theft of the cow. He wasn't certain he was prepared to face whatever odd thing Dungal had stumbled across.

Dungal was an awesome spectacle of size and strength. With a single hand he wielded a sword so large that most men couldn't wield it with two. He could lift a bullock completely off the ground as he had proven on several occasions, and in a stand up fight he could clear a gateway or smash a shield wall all by himself. But if the man's strength was remarkable, no less was the simplicity of his mind. The oddest, most mundane things could amuse him for hours to the annoyance of everyone else.

The wet fellow accompanying Dungal didn't appear to offer the prospect that anything interesting might develop from his presence. Where he had come from and why Dungal found him interesting was a mystery.

Dungal didn't offer an explanation, preferring to grin like a fool rather than say anything. The youth beside him did look strangely familiar, but though Bran studied his features, the auburn hair and dark green eyes, recognition eluded him. The stranger said nothing.

After a moment Bran addressed Dungal. "You found him? Then I'll wager it's queer enough, but who in blazes is he?"

Dungal seemed amused. "Ho! Ho! You've got to guess!"

Bran stood up. A dangerous light gleamed in his eyes, and Evan took careful note of his surroundings in case it came to a fight.

"No I don't have to guess. Tell me who he is or I'll kill the pair of you! I'm not playing games in this miserable weather! Who the devil are you?"

"We've met before," offered Evan, "though neither of us profited from the meeting."

"Riddles! Riddles!" fumed Bran.

"Kevin Mac Maoilorian," offered Evan.

"Who?"

"The bowman, Bran," laughed Dungal. "It's the bowman!"

Bran's eyes widened and a shiver rushed up his spine. "What are you doing here? Dungal killed you. Why aren't you dead?"

Dungal laughed merrily. "His God is merciful!"

"I'd argue the point," snarled the bandit leader. "What do you want with us now? Haven't you caused enough trouble?"

"All I really want is food," said Evan apologetically.

"Food? You're bad luck bowman, and just now we can't stand anymore bad luck, d'ya hear? Get out of here before somebody kills you and brings the wrath of your God down on us again!"

Dungal flung his arm around Evan.

"We can't send him away hungry. It might make his God angry ya know?"

Bran glared at Dungal but didn't have the courage to disagree. He would have liked nothing better than to kill the boy himself and have done with it, but he didn't dare. He was haunted by the idea that his troubles were a direct result of hurting this youth to begin with. Perhaps if he were kind he might get Iosa Christus off his back.

"Fine! Eat! Have some wine! Then begone and take your God with you!"

The meal was the best Evan could ever remember though it consisted of nothing more than undercooked beef and cheap, sour wine. The rain stopped midway through the repast, the clouds dispersed and the sun appeared, lending cheery warmth to the newly freshened air. By the time he licked the last traces of grease from his fingers he was satisfied and content, if still wet.

Dungal begged to know everything that had happened to Evan, or as he knew him, Kevin, since their first unfortunate meeting. Evan was happy to share the information, though he wasn't entirely forthcoming. He spoke of the reunion with his brother, but left out the fact that his brother was the High King of Glenmara. He didn't say anything about Aine or Durham, but he did explain that he was heading to Gwenferew, though he mentioned nothing about goblins.

In return, Dungal recited the litany of unfortunate events that had befallen him and his companions since they left Glenne. Evan listened politely, but without interest until the tale came to Moloch's temple. Bran didn't think this little history lesson either necessary or wise until he noticed how agitated Evan became at the mention of the place. The conversation was getting interesting.

"When the Legion shows up, Bran says 'Time to go!' and go we does. We ain't fool enough to fight the Legion!"

"And what happened?" demanded Evan. "What happened to the High Priest and the girl he brought with him?"

Dungal shrugged. "How should I know? Once we sees the Legion lined up on the ridge we just grabbed the horses afore somebody else got 'em."

"Yeah," said another brigand, "Nobody wanted to dance with the Legion. Them priests wasn't paying enough fer that, d'ya see?"

The man speaking might have been happier to cut Evan's throat than engage in polite conversation with his one-time enemy had Dungal not been close at hand. But the big man seemed genuinely fond of the young bowman, and no one dared cross him.

Evan continued to inquire about Aine and whether the Legion had rescued her, but no one seemed to know.

"What difference do it make?" muttered Dungal, unable to comprehend why Evan should care about such things, "Either the Legion won or the Priests won. Either that girl is dead or she's alive. Anyway, we're safe."

"What do you care about that girl anyway?" asked Bran. "Rumor had it she was a Baron's daughter and wouldn't have bothered to look at the likes of us anyhow. What about you bowman? Taken table with the King lately?"

The little crowd laughed, but Evan didn't think it funny. "All I know about the girl is what I've heard here," he lied. "It's just a shame to see those priests . . ." He couldn't finish his statement.

"Ah, why worry?" consoled Bran, his eyes flashing with merriment, "The doxy no doubt deserves whatever she gets."

"What would you know about her?" Evan snarled, and his hand strayed to his sword hilt. "You could never rise to her station!"

The bandits around the fire stiffened and looked nervously about. No one spoke to Bran like that.

But Bran only smiled. "Rise did you say? Rise to consort with those who lick the boots of the king? No, I'll never rise that high. And if I know nothing about that girl then neither do you, so keep a civil tongue in your head or you'll lose them both."

Evan looked into Bran's cold eyes, nodded and looked into the fire.

Content for the moment, Bran tossed Evan a wine-sack. There was more to Kevin Mac Maoilorian than he was telling. Why was he so defensive about a girl he claimed to know nothing about? Why was the pommel of his sword set with semi-precious stones and chased in gold filigree?

By now it was dark and the air had become chill. Evan huddled closer to the fire wondering if he would survive the night. Whatever happened, he didn't think he would get much sleep. The air no longer smelled fresh. The gentle breeze carried an incredible stench. Even the hardened outlaws began complaining about it. And it was getting worse.

***

Dawn heralded its arrival with a splash of orange so violent that it appeared the sky had burst into flame. Evan struggled with himself as he watched the bandits prepare their ponies. They were about to ride into a maelstrom unawares. So he told them about the goblins.

"Goblins?" laughed Bran. "What stories you tell! Save them for children."

"I don't tell stories," Evan insisted.

"Don't you?"

Evan gritted his teeth. The man had called him a liar! Still, it wouldn't do to be killed over an insult. "You'll see soon enough," he mumbled.

"You've seen goblins?" Dungal asked, his eyes wide, voice full of wonder.

"Yes," Evan replied amidst the chuckles and guffaws of the others.

"What does they look like?"

"Like yerself!" someone cried.

"Nah! He's an ogre!"

"I'll break yer head!" Dungal warned, rounding on his tormentors.

"Save it for the goblins!" Bran chortled.

Dungal returned to Evan's side. "Don't pay no mind to them others. I believes ya. I'd like ta see a goblin someday."

"I fear you'll soon get the chance."

"Well, we're going the same way, so why doesn't ya ride with us?"

"Oh yes!" snorted Bran. "Do come along. It'll be such fun."

Well fed and rested, the little band slowly wended its way north. As they drew near the bridge that would take them across the river to Gwenferew, Bran's apprehension peaked. It was the only way to Dhub, but the path would bring them uncomfortably close to Legion Provosts. Both Bran and Dungal were well known among the Gwenferew detachment and would be easily recognized.

Dungal said little the entire morning, content to ride beside Evan in silence. Sometime just before the sun reached its zenith, the big man turned to his companion. "Bowman," he ventured, his voice quiet and full of question, "you was merciful to me once. D'ya think yer God would be merciful to me?"

"Of course," Evan assured him, and Dungal nodded and said nothing more.

The road turned sharply toward the river as it rose toward a large, treeless plateau from which they would be able to see Gwenferew. Soon they would cross the bridge.

But then from the trees bordering the river came the unmistakable sound of battle accompanied by a strange droning noise that only Evan recognized. Bran was in no mood to investigate. Whatever was going on in the woods was no concern of his. His luck had been bad enough without courting disaster. Besides, the bowman, the harbinger of all the misfortune that had been visited upon them, was in their midst. He urged his horse up the slope.

A woman's scream spun Evan's head around and an instant later the same voice cried out in a single desperate word.

"Eowulf!"

The blood coursing through his body was replaced with a rush of fear so intense that it took his breath away. For he knew that voice, and found himself charging down the hill toward the shadowed forest.

Like a hunted animal, Eowulf kept moving, dragging Aine with him until lack of food and the effects of exhaustion forced them to halt. He purposefully avoided settlements, fearful of being run to ground and captured by foes both real and imaginary. Finally, when the horse collapsed and died the pair stopped in a forest glade beside the River Cuinn and slept like dead things.

Eowulf was in the thrall of dreams before his eyes were fully closed and these lasted until he opened them again nearly a full day later. They were tortured, angry dreams, hinting at the promise of happiness without ever delivering. They were dreams of Durham, of Anwend Halfdane, of Claranides and the ruin that had overtaken his life. And there were dreams of Aine.

Aine Ceallaigh, the only hope of any happiness left to him, filled his sleep with a tantalizing presence. He longed for her, willing that she come to him, love him as he had come to love her, but she remained aloof, removed, beyond attaining.

She smiled and it was as though he had never known pain or sorrow, all of it swept away by the power of her joy. But then she was drowning, dragged into the cold water by something dark, selfish, and evil and Eowulf knew that he was the darkness.

He tried to reach her, but she slipped away, and the harder he tried, the farther away she moved. She laughed at him, and he couldn't save her. She was beyond him, always out of reach. To possess her he would have to destroy her.

Eowulf woke with a start, his mind still filled with the terror and despair of his dream. He shook his head, took a deep, ragged breath and ran his hands over his face.

It had been raining when they dragged themselves beneath this huge oak tree, but now the sky was a pallet of brilliant blue. Balancing the pleasantness of the setting was the remarkable stench that hung in the air like a fog.

Aine still slept, lying in the grass at the foot of the tree. She was dirty, her hair knotted and tangled, her clothing torn and disheveled and Eowulf found her as beautiful now as when she had sung that remarkable song in the banquet hall of the Sceir Naid a lifetime ago.

His dream troubled him. He wanted Aine more than he wanted life, but his boundless desire and uncontrolled passion could easily destroy what he most desired. He had to be careful, gentle and patient until she softened toward him.

But then a revelation burst upon him with the instantaneous power of a thunderclap. *She had come back for him.* She had ridden back into the temple and saved him from certain death. She could have left him there and been free, but she had come back. She did care for him! What more evidence did he need? What she wouldn't say in words she expressed plainly enough when she spurred her horse back into the temple yard.

Eowulf smiled. He'd been blind. The silly girl was actually fond of him. And why shouldn't she be? He had been good to her, saved her life, and protected her from those treacherous priests. What woman wouldn't appreciate that?

He sat down beside the sleeping girl. What a comfort she was now that he had lost everything. Leaning down, he kissed her.

For an instant she seemed to respond, moving beneath him as if glad to be embraced, but the illusion vanished when she slapped him hard across the face. He recoiled, but as Aine tried to get up he shoved her back down.

"What's the matter with you?" he snarled, trying to kiss her again. "It's me, Eowulf."

She didn't calm down. From the moment of her abduction she had feared this more than any other eventuality, and now that fear leant strength to her exhausted body. Yet Eowulf was stronger still and forced his lips against her own. She screamed into his face, tried to bite him, kicked and struggled and fought with all her might.

Fueled by a terrible longing and an uncontrollable rage, Eowulf tightened his grip on the prize. He slapped her, bloodying her lips, and the sudden splash of crimson across her face was enough to give him pause. Rage gave way to crushing remorse. He released her as though he were in pain.

Aine scrambled to her feet, bracing herself against the tree. If she ran he would catch her so she determined to fight. Whether she won or lost, lived or died, she would never submit.

Yet Eowulf remained on his knees, his head between his hands as though he had been struck a vicious blow. He knew what was happening. As in his dream he was pulling Aine down into the dark depths of his rage where nothing could live.

"Go before I kill you, Biscuit," he said in despair. "I don't want to hurt you, but I will"

Aine's heart softened. He was a dangerous man, yet she pitied him.

"Go Biscuit," he snarled. "Or I'll take you and then kill myself."

"Then turn to Iosa and turn your back on the man you have been," she blurted out. Within his tortured soul a thread of conscience remained, the slightest bit of sanity and goodness that held the evil at bay. If only she could reach it before he was forever lost to the darkness! But Eowulf wouldn't listen.

"Shut up! Stop pushing me! Leave now or I won't be able to keep my promise."

Aine took a step back and glanced over her shoulder. She didn't trust him, but something kept her there. "Turn to Iosa, Eowulf Fitzwarren, and be saved."

His eyes glared ice. "Be saved? Nothing can save me, and nothing can save you either. I warned you, didn't I? Didn't I? What did you expect?"

"I expected you to act like a man, not like an animal that cannot control itself. Where is your honor? Where is your decency? I have seen the goodness in your heart. Cling to that!"

"Decency? Honor? Those words mean nothing! You don't get by with decency and honor. People understand force, brutal, remorseless power," he snarled. "Your god is for weaklings and simpletons. He's a fairy tale!"

Trembling, Aine shook her finger at Eowulf. "Are you blind? Brush aside your pride and passion and think of everything that brought us to this moment. The Chapel on the Sceir Naid, the gate where your wicked plans fell in pieces before your eyes, the Temple where the Hand of God brought the Legion to our rescue. These things are facts, not fairy tales."

Eowulf spat. "I care nothing for your God."

"Whatever you think of Him, He loves you."

"Loves me?" Eowulf laughed, "What nonsense! I don't love Him! I don't love anything . . . except you, Biscuit."

Aine's eyes flashed. "What sort of love embraces abduction and brutality? There is no love in trying to possess another as you would a horse or a hawk! I don't respond to that sort of love."

"I tried being friendly, and you wanted nothing to do with me. What choice did I have?"

"I do not love you Eowulf Fitzwarren! Can't you understand that?"

"But your God loves me? What sense does that make?"

"It's a different type of love."

"Different? I'm the middle son; I've always measured love by the lack of it! But there was something different about you, something hopeful, and I've nearly destroyed you too. How can God love me?"

Aine wondered the same thing. Yet she knew that this man, so tied to the darkness in his soul that it threatened to destroy everything around him, was still a child of God. "I don't know how. But He loves you so much that He died for you."

The expression on Eowulf's face abruptly changed from disbelief and pain to grim resignation and focused purpose. Aine's blood chilled as a savage emptiness filled his eyes.

"Come here, pretty Biscuit," he said rising. He held one hand out to her while the other slid the sword from his belt in the fluid movement of a practiced warrior.

Aine looked over her shoulder and saw them. More than a dozen misshapen grey forms came swaying out of the forest, whispering to each other in a strange unsettling tongue. She stumbled back into Eowulf who had come up behind her.

"What are they?" she asked, but Eowulf didn't hear her. There was a terrible smile on his face. The appearance of these creatures had saved Aine from his madness, and now he would save her from them, whatever they were.

On they came, chanting a strange droning chorus that echoed dully from the trees like an angry hive of bees.

"Ulu! Ulu! Ulu!"

They spread out, trying to encircle their prey, and Eowulf decided to take the fight to them. Beyond all else that he was, bully, brute and braggart, he was also a warrior.

He bounded forward like an eager acrobat, feinted toward one of the beasts and drove his blade into another. The thing screamed and fell to the forest floor. The others converged on him in their strange swaying gait, hissing and snarling. Despite their clumsy appearance, they were remarkably quick and agile. Steel rang as he parried a blow then another and a third. His own blade found mark again and again and such was his prowess that he might have killed them all had Aine not screamed.

Eowulf turned. She was searching for a weapon, trying to evade the long, thin arms of the grey monster that pursued her, and at the sight Fitzwarren lost focus of anything else. He slashed his way through the closing circle of goblins and struck down the one that threatened Aine, but as he had already marked, his enemies were faster than they appeared. Before he could turn again, goblin steel pierced him through.

Aine screamed out his name as he staggered from the deadly blow, and though he managed to cut down the creature that had killed him, in the next instant he fell to the ground.

The goblins turned toward Aine. She flung herself into the low branches of the oak tree, but as she tried to scramble to safety, a grey hand seized her foot.

She pulled with all her strength, kicked and screamed, yet couldn't pull free. Another hand clawed at her waist and then another and she was flung down into the midst of the foul smelling, gibbering crowd. She screamed again as they prodded and pulled at her.

Then, keeping in common with a morning where sudden and unexpected things seemed to spring from the very earth itself, one of the creatures uttered a frantic cry. In the next instant his grotesque head separated from his misshapen body in an arch of scarlet spray.

With screams of dismay the remainder scattered before the attack of a single unexpected foe whose prowess and savagery were so precise that four of their companions were soon convulsing on the ground. The survivors fled into the trees screeching and wailing.

Aine scrambled to her feet as her rescuer turned from his pursuit. Breath seized in her throat and a terrible trembling overcame her, for it was Evan MacKeth who strode toward her. She tried to call his name but couldn't muster the voice or the strength to speak, and then he was holding her in powerful arms, and she thought she would swoon from the overwhelming relief and joy.

"Sweet Aine," he declared, "the Hand of God Himself has led me to thee." Their lips met, and it was as though they kissed for the first time.

"How?" she said after a moment, "Look at you. How did you find me? Look at you!" She broke into uncontrollable sobs.

"Shhh, shhh, my Sweet," comforted Evan. "The world has gone right side up again and the power of the Living God surrounds us."

"Evan. Dear Evan!"

They clung to each other, but soon the surrounding world began to intrude.

"Who are *they*?" whispered Aine, and Evan saw that Bran Mael Morda's bandits had entered the clearing.

"Did ya see, Bran? Goblins," grunted Dungal, prodding at one of the dead things with the point of his sword. "They stink!"

"I told you there were goblins. I don't tell stories."

Bran chuckled. "Don't you? Then why would a boy named Kevin who claims he doesn't know the girl from Moloch's Temple, now be embracing that same girl and she calling him by an entirely different name. Who are you boy?"

Evan gave a thin smile. "We must follow proper protocol," he said, kissing Aine's hand. "Lady Aine Ceallaigh, may I present Bran Mael Morda and his illustrious company. This large fellow is Dungal."

"The man you fought?" marveled Aine. "The one who wounded you?"

Dungal's face broadened into a smile at being the subject of such a remembrance.

"The same. And this, *gentlemen*, is the Lady Aine Ceallaigh, daughter of Baron Brendan Ceallaigh, sister of Queen Ivrian Murchadha. And I . . . but you tell them m'lady lest I be accused of telling stories again."

Aine boldly declared, "He is Evan MacKeth, brother of High King Osric Murchadha of Glenmara."

The bandits stared. Some squinted their eyes as if trying to visually discern something royal about the pair. Dungal laughed with delight. But Bran found nothing funny in this turn of events.

If their luck had been bad before, now they had been cursed. The king's brother? It wasn't enough that every bounty hunter, local sheriff and the Legion Provost were after them. If anything bad happened to Evan MacKeth while in their company there would be nowhere in the world they could hide. So when Bran heard one of his men mention hostages and ransom, he grabbed the unfortunate fellow and threw him down.

"There won't be any hostages! These two are free to go about their business. We have enough troubles without adding to the pot."

"What about them?" asked Dungal gesturing to the trees.

The forest had come alive with grey goblins, hundreds of them moving methodically toward the little knot of humans.

"Well, well," snarled Bran rounding on Dungal, "are you satisfied now, you great clumsy oaf? You had to come chasing after your friend, and now that lot is after us. Can it get worse?"

"Of course I followed him," countered Dungal. "He's the King's brother ain't he?"

"But you didn't know that! If your wit was half as vast as your stature you'd rule the world!"

Unaware he had been insulted, Dungal grinned. This was turning into a wonderful day. The bowman was a royal, this pretty little girl had appeared, and now there were all these grey fellows to fight. A wonderful day indeed!

"They'll surround us if we stay here," offered Evan, "We'd do better atop the ridge."

Bran gave an exaggerated bow. "After you, m'lord!"

Evan laughed. "To the horses!"

"Wait!" Aine cried. She hurried to the place where Eowulf had fallen and brushed his cold cheek with her hand.

"Poor tormented soul. He saved me," she said, tears standing in her eyes. "As surely as you saved me and the One True God saved us both."

"Then I will honor his memory for your sake, Sweet Aine."

"Touching," hissed Bran, "but we'll join him if we don't go now!"

They hurried back to their horses and galloped to the summit of the bare ridge where the land fell away north and south. Beyond the winding course of the River Cuinn the town of Gwenferew loomed up from the landscape, and even from such distance it was apparent that something was wrong. A good portion of the town stood in ruins.

"Blood of the Gods!" cursed Bran. "What else? What's going on?"

"I told you," said Evan, "There are goblins from here to the mountains. We've got to get into the town."

"In a pig's eye! You go to the town, or to blazes for all I care. We're going back where we came from!"

"If you must," said Evan, gesturing at the swarm of goblins that had emerged to block the south road. Soon the northern road was similarly occupied. Distant drums sounded, their deep resonance displacing the air with fear.

Across the river goblin banners fluttered above a ring of newly constructed earthworks that spread out across the rolling meadows of tall grass that men called Clon Miarth. From the bordering forest an army charged down upon the goblin fortifications, and though Evan couldn't make out the heraldry on the banner they followed, the color of uniforms and the blazon on shields announced that the Royal Household of Murchadha had come to Gwenferew.

"It's Osric!" Evan enthused.

Yet though overjoyed that his brother had broken the siege at Durham, though he marveled at the events that had brought them to this place at this moment, Evan despaired at what he witnessed now. Osric's tiny force was arrayed against a goblin host many times its size. They would never break the defensive line. Of more immediate concern, Evan and his companions found themselves cut off from the town, isolated on the high ridge overlooking the wide, treacherous river.

Bran cursed and shook his head. "Well bow-man, you've killed us all this time. How your God must hate me!"

"He doesn't hate you, Bran."

"Since I met you I've been hounded from one disaster to the next—like a sheep being herded to the shearing pens."

Evan grinned. "The Lord is my Shepherd, so we're not sheared yet. He didn't lead us here to die on this barren hill."

"No," said Aine, arms flung tightly about Evan, "I've seen too many miracles to lose faith now."

"If your God can get us out of this I'll think more kindly of Him."

"The river then?" asked Evan, his eyes glinting with excitement.

Bran smiled. "Aye, the river it is you wild man! Come on! We're going for a swim!"

With a wild shout they thundered down the hill toward the shining ribbon of the River Cuinn.

CHAPTER VI
ARMAGEDDON

The journey to Gwenferew proved long and torturously slow. With little time to recover from the battle that had saved the kingdom, Osric and his battered army turned north with the first rays of the new day.

Osric chose a route along the western bank of the Cuinn through good, open country to the fortified Manor of Morleigh Dunroon. Here he could feed and shelter his army in preparation for the final two-day journey to Gwenferew.

With him came most of the able bodied men from the city, the Provisional Militia from Faltigern and the lion's share of Duke Eiolowen's retainers who had followed Padraigh to Durham. Too injured to travel, Padraigh Rinn stayed behind to organize the defense of the Capital.

Anwend Halfdane and his wild Varangians gladly journeyed north too. They considered it the height of hospitality that the King had arranged a war for them, and having whetted their appetites in Durham, they were anxious to find other diversions for their swords. Forcibly adopted, a reluctant Martin Reamon accompanied them.

They marched toward Gwenferew, King Osric, Duke Dunroon, Anwend Halfdane, Martin

Reamon and just over two thousand others. Tired, battered and poorly provisioned they made their way toward the beleaguered city. There was no time to prepare a proper logistics train, so with whatever provisions they could throw together, strap to their saddles or carry on their backs, the rag-tag army made its way north. North to Gwenferew.

After a week of steady travel the advance guard crested a ridgeline of low hills and looked out over the manor lands of Duke Morleigh Dunroon. What remained of the village and the fortified Long House were as many piles of charred wood and blackened stone. Corpses, both human and goblin, dotted the scorched sward like evil-smelling flowers.

They found no survivors, and great was Morleigh's grief. Although his wife and children were safe in Durham, his parents and many loyal friends and retainers had perished. Anwend Halfdane laid a hand on Morleigh's shoulder and made a terrible promise.

"For each of your dead upon this field I will repay your enemies a hundred fold."

It was scant comfort to Dunroon, but he was glad that Anwend was his friend.

With his intended base of operations destroyed, Osric considered his options. Without provisions the army couldn't remain in the field, and unless they could force a decisive battle with the goblins, their ability to fight would continue to diminish until they would have to turn back.

They had just begun to bury the dead when drums began to sound from the surrounding forests. Soon Osric's cavalry reported a large force of goblins approaching from the north. The king anchored the center of his line on the ruins of Dunroon Manor, massed his cavalry on the far right and waited for the enemy to arrive.

The goblin chieftain Runamok had marched south at Ugrik's bidding, and by his hand Dunroon Manor had been laid waste. Preparing to march back to Gwenferew, scouts brought word of the approaching human army. He sent a blocking force to neutralize the cavalry, strengthened his right and drove hard against the human left. In a few moments the human line began to fold back toward the manor.

Osric watched the battle unfold. Though outnumbered, the goblins were rested and well fed. They fought well too, exhibiting determined discipline and frightening ferocity. Goblins screeched and gibbered as they threw themselves against the opposing wall of steel and human flesh. The terrible thunder of their drums and the wild ululation of their battle cry struck fear into the hearts of Osric's men. The human line wavered.

Osric's cavalry tried to overrun the goblin left, but with practiced precision, their formations became bristling hedges of spears that the horses would not approach.

Fear began to give way to panic as the struggle on the left reached its peak. Osric's army was exhausted, hungry and ill prepared for the horror of the goblin host. The drums, the strange cries, the remarkable stench, the orange eyes and grey flesh were overpowering. Sensing the imminent collapse of their enemies, the goblins strove harder and the human line began to collapse, but while the army fell apart, Anwend Halfdane and his Varangians held their ground.

"You'd better do something," Otho admonished Ragnar.

"Do something? What have I been doing if not something? What did you have in mind?"

"Something more severe. They'll break our line."

"No they won't," insisted Ragnar. "I've never seen a goblin before, but they've never seen a Berserk."

Many warriors might reach that state of agitation and anger that pushed them beyond pain, wounds and fatigue, but they weren't Berserks. Being a Berserk wasn't something you could learn; it was something you were born into. It was a state of physical abandon where the body was overcome by the lust of battle and the heady, dangerous desire to spill blood. And though this spell often came upon Ragnar unbidden, he knew how to urge it along.

He thought of the dead women and children, the twisted, tortured bodies of those who had fallen into the hands of the soul-less creatures that were now trying to kill the rest of them. He recalled every wicked thing that had ever occurred to him, every slight, cruelty and injustice that he had experienced since he was a boy, and every goblin that fell to his crimson washed sword drove the passion higher.

It came upon him in a wave of savagery and rage, consuming every vestige of his humanity, until he was more animal than man. Once gripped in this madness, only death would stop him.

Now because of Ragnar and those that followed in his wake, the goblins began to give ground. Humans, who moments before had been in retreat, resumed their attack with renewed vigor. At the same time Brendan Ceallaigh rallied his cavalry, wheeled east as if to withdraw and then turned on the pursuing enemy. Goblin discipline fell apart at the first shock of horseflesh, and within moments they were fleeing for the refuge of the forest.

By the time pursuit was called off, more than five hundred goblins lay dead beneath the darkening sky. Osric's army had suffered a handful dead and a few more wounded, but how easily things had been different without the mad bravery of Ragnar. As if in testimony to the miraculous nature of his triumph, neither he nor any of the Varangians had been so much as scratched.

Yet victory carried its own cost, and payment came in the condition of the men. They were exhausted and demoralized, facing a long march without food and a hard fight at road's end. Many of Osric's nobles counseled retreat. The army had been fighting or marching for the past two weeks. Gwenferew would have to hold out until a proper army could be raised and equipped. Anyway, there was a Legion garrison there. Let the Legion handle it. Nothing would be gained by throwing away lives in pointless heroics, especially since Duke Laighan was still at large with an army of his own. The civil war was only beginning

But Osric didn't view the rebellion of his Dukes and the events in Gwenferew as unrelated. They were of one cloth, woven together in blood by the spirits that would glory in the destruction of Iosa's faithful. Claranides and his brood were but puppets in a larger play whose first act was barely done. The curtain had risen on act two, and the stage was full of Shadow Creatures. If there were to be a final act, Osric would write it to the glory of his God. He couldn't do that if he went back to Durham.

"In the morning I march north. If you are too timid to follow, run home to your women and cross my path no more. When this is over, I will remember who stood with me and who did not. Now rest. We will need all our strength soon."

In the morning the army moved on. Despite the grumbling, no one wished to desert the king. Still, with their greatest battle before them, morale continued to plummet.

———

The battered remnants of Runamok's command straggled into the encampment at Gwenferew with word of the approaching humans.

Ugrik knew he couldn't keep his army on campaign much longer. In spite of their success, the plunder and slaves they had taken, they were running out of supplies. It was bad enough having to eat human food, and even that was in short supply. Still, he wasn't going back to the mountain with the Legion garrison intact. It would take a few more days to complete the tunnels and then goblins would emerge inside the fortress to destroy everything that was left in the man-town. But before that, he would deal with the rabble marching toward him.

———

It took two long, agonizing days for Osric's army to travel from Dunroon Manor to the edges of Clon Miarth. They arrived late of an afternoon in the midst of a daylong downpour. Thunder echoed like monstrous drums across the sodden fields. Lightning hissed in tongues of molten silver, etched among the dreary, rain-swollen clouds.

The army huddled beneath their cloaks, hungry and hesitant. Many had fallen on the march, too sick, too weak, too weary to continue, leaving the ragged ranks thin. It was a sad army indeed that came at last to Clon Miarth.

Darkness came early, clouds and rain obscuring the sun before it was fully set. Osric posted pickets, and the army waited for morning.

———

Dawn presented an amazing contrast to the dismal darkness of the previous night. A remarkable canvas of blue sky stretched beyond the river and mountains as if confirming the notion that hope yet remained. Yet clear skies and bright sunlight also revealed a grim and cheerless sight.

Gwenferew stood completely encircled by a ring of earthen redoubts and deep ditches. Large sections of the town wall had been dismantled, and the materials used to construct the defensive line now blocking Osric's way. Beneath crude banners, thousands of goblin warriors manned the works, and though the flag of the Second Glenmaran Border Legion still flew above the citadel in the town, Osric despaired of ever reaching it.

How could his men overcome such an obstacle? How could they prevail against such numbers? Amid the jeers and howls of the watching goblins, Osric led his army into the bordering forest.

Atop a small hill in the middle of his defensive line, Ugrik frowned. He was disappointed that the human men would slink away without a fight, but he was hardly surprised. With such a small army it would be madness to attack a fortified position. He toyed with the idea of pursuing them but thought better of it. He'd have soldiers spread out from here to there if he allowed them to chase after. As it was there were still goblins cavorting about on the far side of the river despite his best efforts to recall them.

He was mulling this over when the human army charged out of the forest with a roar. For a moment Ugrik was alarmed, but then he smiled and laughed. Let them come. Such a rabble was but an inconsequential thing to mighty Ugrik and his goblin host. He would swat them like an annoying insect and turn to other things.

In the Legion fortress, the tower sentry reported to the Officer of the Watch and within moments Giomer had been summoned.

"It's the king, Domini!" the officer enthused.

"It won't matter who it is if we don't help them," rejoined Giomer. "They'll never break that line. Officers to my quarters now!"

On the plain below, Osric himself led the attack. Leaving the horses in the forest, the human army charged out of the trees and crashed against the great redoubt that the goblins had built on the slopes of the little hill known as the Tor Mort.

The Tor Mort. The Hill of Death, so named for the ruinous battle fought on its slopes over three centuries before, where invading Ascalonian Legions defeated the combined forces of the united Glenmaran tribes. That day fourteen chieftains died on that insignificant bit of topography, forever and tragically fixing the Tor in Glenmaran history. But if the hill was insignificant in geographical terms, strategically it was of the greatest importance.

The goblins had made it the center of their defensive line, constructing a huge redoubt at the summit from which the rest of the fortifications branched east and north. If the Tor could be taken it might be possible to roll up the goblins' flanks, sending them scurrying back to their dark holes. But it was a desperate audacity to pit such small numbers against such a mighty foe.

The human army clambered across the shallow ditch and clawed its way up the hill, pulling and chopping at the abatis of sharpened stakes that barred their way. A steady hail of spears and rocks rained down into the attackers, and even though the goblins lacked bows, casualties began to mount long before the humans came to grips with their opponents. Those that managed to get past the barricades ran headlong into a solid wall of goblins and were sent reeling back wounded and dying. For if Osric had correctly surmised that the Tor was the key to victory, Ugrik recognized it too, and it was the most heavily fortified spot in the line. Goblins crowded the slopes beneath the banner of their mighty chieftain.

The attack began to spread left and right as the main effort crashed against and split apart on the Tor Mort. Like a wave thrusting against a rocky shore, it dashed itself into foam and spray. They would never win the day unless they could concentrate their effort on a single point.

More men struggled across the ditch and up the hill, stumbling over the dead and wounded. Osric reached the goblin line with a handful of others and strove to cut his way through to the interior of the redoubt, but there were too many goblins. Killing one or ten seemed to have no effect on the solid wall of grey.

Soldiers leapt into the muddy morass of the ditch, softened by the rain and churned into a deepening bog by hundreds of passing feet. It slowed their rush to a crawl and bottled them up as they ascended the hill. Those that managed to reach the actual battle were met with a seemingly impregnable line of goblins screaming their war cry above the thunder of massive drums. BOOM BOOM! BOOM BOOM! BOOM - A - BOOM! BOOM - A - BOOM!

"ULU! ULU! ULU!"

The humans threw themselves against the goblin defenses hoping that by supreme effort they might somehow breach the line. But the goblins were rested and fed while Osric's stalwarts were nearly spent and starving. They had but one chance for victory, and if they fell back now that chance would disappear.

In the ditch beneath the redoubt where the blood trickling down the hill had turned the mud into scarlet slush, Anwend Halfdane called his Varangians together. "If we don't take this hill we're dead men," he said over the tumult of battle. "They will soon strike at our flanks, and if they catch us here we'll be slaughtered. So break that line my brave boys and pull down that goblin banner. Five hundred marks of gold to he that brings it down!"

With a tremendous shout the Varangians charged up the Tor. The renewed effort pushed the goblins back, and suddenly humans were inside the redoubt, tearing apart the goblin formation. Reinforcements rushed in to dislodge them.

In the town the gates of the Legion fortress burst open and the plaza filled with troops. They were instantly intercepted by goblins, and a sharp battle ensued to keep the Legion inside the town.

Yet as Klabaga threw his troops against the Legion, his mind was occupied with something else. Every time he tried to concentrate on the battle at hand, the coarse hair on the back of his neck bristled. The human boy Evan MacKeth was very close now; he was swimming the river.

And indeed he was. Faced with the goblins on the far bank of the Cuinn, Evan, Aine and Bran Mael Morda's bandits went into the river, horses and all. The current pulled them swiftly along as they clung to their swimming mounts.

Evan's gaze locked with Aine. There was such sweet beauty in her face, such love in her eyes that he began to cry. "I thought I had lost you," he said.

"Foolish boy," she replied, smiling through her own tears, "it's never you'll lose me."

They came ashore scattered along a muddy beach a mile south of where they had entered the river. Soon they were riding north. Though the outlaws complained about their wet clothing, no one had been lost to the treacherous waters.

Yet being safely across presented another set of difficulties. Battle raged just ahead; Bran heard the sounds of slaughter through the trees. And although Evan MacKeth and Dungal seemed anxious to join the fray, Bran had no intention of getting involved. He enjoyed a fight as much as anyone, but now wasn't the time.

Ragnar enjoyed a good fight too. He hadn't been so happy since he left Varangia. The previous battles had been but appetizers to this, the real feast. The humans still held the edge of the redoubt on the Tor Mort, and while they sought to push the goblins out, the goblins strove to retake what they had lost. Corpses began to pile up in horrible drifts, but the fight went on atop the dead and wounded.

From atop the Tor, Ugrik sent messengers scurrying to other parts of the line. The human men pressed the redoubt, and more struggled up the mud slick slopes of the hill. Behind him the Legion waged a bloody battle for egress from the town.

"Tear that cursed banner down!" roared Morleigh Dunroon as he hacked and stabbed and battered his way forward. "It will not fly over my lands!"

Again and again the men hurled themselves into the mass of grey atop the tiny hill, and just as it had on that day over three hundred years before, blood ran like a crimson flood on the Tor Mort. They pushed the goblins back to the final slope of the hill, but Runamok was already leading a force to take Osric's army in the flank. From his command post Ugrik saw them hurrying down the muddy road. Anwend Halfdane saw them coming too and knew that nothing could save them now apart from taking the hill, and even that might not be enough.

Cresting the ridge as the road rose then fell to the valley of Clon Miarth, the panorama of battle unfolded before Evan MacKeth. It was a spectacle beyond anything he had ever witnessed, both beautiful and terrible. The sound rose like the deadly song of a siren, luring men to their destruction. His eyes brightened, for he knew that amidst the carnage he would find Klabaga.

Then he saw Runamok's goblins. "Get off the horse," he ordered Aine.

She boxed his ears. "Why? So you may charge down there and leave me alone?"

"It isn't safe . . ."

"Nor is being kidnapped and dragged over half the kingdom, but I survived that. Just give me a weapon and off we go!"

"Aine, it is madness to go."

"Here sweet lady," offered Dungal and handed her a fearsome axe he unstrapped from his saddle. "See if this fits your wee hand."

She took it with a smile, and in attempting to swing it, nearly struck Evan in the head.

"What're you doing Dungal?" asked Bran as though he were talking to a mischievous child. "We're not going down there."

"The king's brother wants to go," he said simply, "and his sweet lady, so I'll go too."

"Fight for the king? If you win he'll put you on a gallows, and you won't win. Look out there!"

Even Dungal could tell there were too many goblins and not enough men. He shrugged. "Maybe so, but if the bowman goes, I go."

"And for any that follow I will speak of them to the king," offered Evan, "and plead their case before his court."

Some of Bran's men looked at each other as if considering the offer until Bran roared like a wounded bull. "You'll all die!" he raged. "Look for yourselves. How will he speak for you when your bones are bleaching in the sun?"

"Then stay!" yelled Evan drawing his sword. "Run away and hide like children, but what you behold will rise up and sniff you out and drag you from your hiding places. It is the Lord of Shadows come to destroy us all." With that he charged down the ridge. Like a faithful dog, Dungal followed.

Startled goblins alerted Runamok to the approaching horsemen, and although there were only two, he took no chances. He had barely escaped his previous battle with human cavalry chasing after him. He ordered his troops to form square.

Some tried to obey. But others, many of whom had seen what horses could do at Dunroon Manor, fled for the safety of their fortifications. Two horsemen had stopped the goblins from reaching Osric's flank, but the goblin formation held fast.

The goblins keeping the Legion in the town also held fast, but only because of superior numbers. Klabaga knew that soldier for soldier, grey goblins couldn't hope to match the legionaries they faced. To ensure the destruction of humankind, he would have to look elsewhere.

Right now, elsewhere was behind him. The aspirations of goblins would never be fulfilled while Evan MacKeth lived, and now the boy had crossed the river and was engaged in combat not far away. Fearing that the human boy might turn the tide of battle, Klabaga left Orglyx in charge and went in search of his foe amidst the desperate battle.

Desperate was an entirely inadequate word to describe the situation on the Tor Mort. Osric's army was bleeding to death on the edge of the goblin redoubt. Yet in giving ground to lure the attackers in and crush them from behind, Ugrik had never counted on two horsemen preventing his flanking troops from reaching the fight. Without their assistance, there was a real danger the human men might take the hill. Anwend Halfdane seized upon the opportunity with vigor.

"Once more and the hill is ours!" he cried and in a frenzy of savagery the Varangians broke through and surged up the hill.

Human men poured through the gap, shoving goblins aside only to run into Ugrik's bodyguard formed up at the crest. Yet such was the impetus of the advance that even these massive goblins staggered back.

In the middle of the press Martin tried to stay on his feet. He was reminded of being caught in the river just before he went over the falls. Wherever the Varangians went, he went, but he was so small that he was constantly being shoved out of the way, unable to get to the forefront of the battle. Now suddenly they were charging up the hill, stumbling over the bodies of the slain.

Ragnar had descended into madness again, indicated by superhuman feats of strength and the disquieting fact that foam was running from the corners of his mouth. Goblins gave way before him or fell with unspeakable wounds and even his own fellows gave him a wider berth than usual. An unwilling Martin was shoved into this gap by those coming up behind.

Up the hill, screams and death all around him, Martin staggered toward the banner of the goblin chieftain at the summit. A madness of sound blended into a single horrendous din that ripped at his senses like the claws of a predatory beast. He was pushed right into Ragnar whose violence had reached such a peak that the frightened youth had to duck down and cover himself with his shield to prevent being injured by the wild fellow.

But as Anwend pushed up the Tor, as Osric and Morleigh rolled the goblin line up and out of the redoubt, as Brendan Ceallaigh launched an attack calculated to carry them out onto the plain beyond, Ugrik's counter-attack hurtled into the human army.

Martin saw the goblins swell over the crest of the Tor Mort, rose up to give warning and was struck down by the edge of Ragnar's shield. Seconds later, Ragnar fell too, and the goblins pushed the men down into the redoubt.

By now Runamok realized that only two horsemen were attacking his column, and he could take care of that threat without the encumbrance of a square. His warriors pushed forward in a milling grey mass trying to close with the humans and overwhelm them.

Evan set heels to horse. As long as he kept the goblins busy, fighting or chasing after, they couldn't attack Osric. But Aine, swinging gamely away with her axe wasn't prepared for the sudden lurch. She tumbled to the ground.

More annoyed than hurt, she leapt to her feet and immediately lay about with the axe. Aine knew nothing of the finer points of hand-to-hand combat. She didn't know why these creatures were here or how any of these strange events had happened in the first place. But she knew that the Hand of Almighty God was in all these things, and she wasn't afraid.

The goblins didn't reach her. Dungal scattered them as he charged into their midst while Evan pulled Aine back into the saddle. But now they found themselves surrounded, outnumbered and unable to escape.

Evan called out to his enemies in the Common Goblin tongue. "Back! Back to your dark holes or I shall kill you all!"

The poor goblins had never before heard a human man speak their language, and if his first words were startling, those that followed sent a jolt of fear through them.

"Look at me!" Evan commanded. "For by my hand was the Glamorth slain. By my hand and the power of Iosa Christus was he thrown down!"

They didn't like this at all. Every goblin had heard of the Glamorth's death at the hands of a human boy in Westerfeld. Now he was in their midst.

They began to mutter among themselves. Those closest to Evan tried to back away as though to touch him would spell their doom. Runamok himself hesitated, reflecting on the security of the nearby earthworks. Thus preoccupied, no one noticed Bran Mael Morda and his bandits until it was too late. Sixteen horsemen slammed into five hundred unprepared goblins and sent them fleeing for their lives.

Driven by a terrible anger, Bran was the first among them. None of this had been his doing. He had run from one fire to the next, each one worse than the last. Now it was goblins (what next!), and Dungal had gone off with the king's brother to certain death.

As far as Bran was concerned, the big fool deserved whatever he got, but his companions didn't agree. Dungal was their good luck charm: he always managed to stumble into something propitious. They had to get him out of harm's way at the very least.

So they charged down the ridge, and Bran was convinced that very soon they would all be dead. Yet the goblins began to disperse long before they ever noticed the horsemen approaching. When Bran's stalwarts crashed into them they scattered like leaves in a strong wind.

And wind it seemed. Had they been ten times their number they couldn't have set the goblins to route with any more efficiency. Within moments the little group of humans found themselves alone on the road.

Route was occurring at the redoubt too. As the goblin counterattack pushed down the Tor, Osric's army began to break apart. The king tried to rally them, to somehow wring a last ounce of effort from his faltering men, but they had nothing left. All that was left was to keep their retreat from becoming a massacre.

The Legion faced its own difficulty. Though disciplined, highly trained soldiers, they couldn't break out of the town. Giomer exhorted his legionaries on, but there were limits to even their legendary prowess.

Ugrik sensed victory as the human army began to retreat. Runamok's column was running, dispersed by a handful of horses, but it didn't matter. The humans were finished.

Amid the tangle of bodies covering the soft sward of the Tor Mort, one figure stirred beneath a pile of corpses. Martin wasn't certain he was alive, for he couldn't see and could scarcely move.

He freed one arm and wiped his hand over his eyes. It came back sticky with blood, but now he could see. Bodies littered the landscape. He discovered he was lying in a thickening pool of blood. He threw up.

Goblins swarmed everywhere. The only humans present lay in motionless heaps on the ground. Close at hand, beneath the goblin banner at the summit of the tor, an enormous goblin gestured with his sword and gave orders that were instantly obeyed.

Martin pulled himself from beneath the dead Varangians, clawing at the caked blood covering his eyes. A voice in his pounding head urged him to lie still, to cover himself with the corpses of the slain. Burrowing into the earth seemed the only way to stay alive amid this carnage, and Martin didn't want to die.

Yet something stronger than fear overcame his frantic desire to simply survive. It was the same something that led him to blow his horn on that death filled morning atop the Sceir Naid, the same something that bid him follow Lord Evan into the river, and that drove him to deliver the message of the dead legionary; duty. If he were to die, it wouldn't be hiding like a frightened child.

The world swirled like a top as he struggled to his feet. His trembling hand clutched the hilt of the dead legionary's sword. Stumbling, staggering, on feet that seemed ready to betray him at any instant, he came up behind the goblin on the hill. Though all about him the battle raged, Martin heard nothing but the steady thud, thud, thud of his pulse that at each beat pumped more blood into his eyes.

Ugrik saw something from the corner of his eye and turned to find a small human boy swaying toward him. Wounded and covered in mud and filth, it appeared too weak to be a threat. Ugrik had decided to kill it himself when a peculiar thing happened.

The goblin chieftain felt a sting in his wrist and was confused to find his sword lying on the ground. He couldn't find his hand. Ugrik tried to call out, but could make no sound, for the small human had stabbed him in the throat. Before he could sort through the confusion he collapsed and died beneath his own banner.

For a moment, Martin steadied himself against the goblin standard, but there was no time to waste. Summoning all his remaining strength he tore free the flag, hurled it to the ground and took up his horn. In clear, powerful notes that rose above the din of battle he played the call "Rally on me!"

Goblin and human alike turned to the summit of the hill where Ugrik's body lay slumped at the feet of the young boy. Even the legionaries battling to break out of the town harkened to the trumpet call and its apparent meaning; Osric had taken the tor.

Both in the town and at the earthworks, goblins, standing fast only moments before, now gave ground. Formations began to fray and dissolve as goblins sought safety elsewhere. The horn continued its call.

"Well you heard it, didn't you?" grunted Giomer. "Rally on the Tor Mort! To the Tor you lazy soldiers! The Tor!"

The legionaries pressed forward with a great roar and the goblins turned and ran. Declining pursuit, Giomer led his men toward Osric's army.

Now the king's men renewed their faltering attack, carried the hill in one violent rush, and planted Osric's banner at the summit. Everywhere on the field goblins abandoned their fortifications and fled west toward the comforting shadow of the forest. Caught up in the unexpected exodus, Klabaga was swept along with them.

Evan MacKeth reined his horse in atop the abandoned goblin earthworks and let out a whoop of joy. The day was won! He turned and kissed a delighted Aine.

Bran corralled his little band like a mother hen gathers her chicks. His men laughed, giddy from their wild ride and the success of their charge. Perhaps the curse of Iosa Christus was broken.

"Farewell bowman," he called. "We've run off your little grey friends and now we'll take our leave. Many thanks for the entertainment!"

Evan chuckled and bowed. "Stay!" he offered. "The party isn't over yet!"

"No thank you, kind sir," replied Bran, "None of us would enjoy the party the Legion has planned. It has something to do with ropes, if you catch my meaning."

"I'll intercede on your behalf."

"I said no, curse your eyes!" Bran snarled. "I've had enough d'ya hear? I'll not hang for you. Even the king doesn't interfere in Legion justice and Legion justice is a rope! Come on Dungal."

But Dungal, sitting proudly next to Evan, hung his head.

"I ain't going Bran," he said sheepishly, a silly grin splayed across his broad face. "I'm staying with the bowman . . . that is, with the young laird here, begging yer pardon."

"Dungal," crooned Bran, "they'll hang you sure and certain. Come with us."

Dungal shook his head. "No, no, I ain't going. I'll stay with the laird."

"I'm honored you'd stay," said Evan, "but he's right. I can speak for you, but it doesn't signify . . ."

Dungal shook his head again. "That don't matter none. It's just I can't leave you now, don't ya see? I can't, that's all, and I won't."

"Then stay and die!" said Bran.

"Goodbye, Bran," Dungal said sadly, but before he could say anything more Bran Mael Morda spat on the ground and spurred his horse west. The others tarried but a moment longer before they too abandoned their companion to his own folly.

Osric's army flooded across the Tor Mort in an irresistible tide, sweeping the goblins from their path like flotsam in a flood. The entire goblin line from the river to the forest was now in full flight, and as the Legion joined with the soldiers of the king they attempted to organize a pursuit. Now was the time to break the enemy once and for all, but the men were spent.

Klabaga's ambitions were falling apart before his eyes; eight thousand goblins fled from a force less than a quarter their size. If they would but turn around they could destroy this rabble. The Red Goblin stopped, planted his feet, and grabbed the first goblin he could reach.

"Stand!" he screamed. "Stand ya foul smelling ditch pigs! D'ya run like frightened she-goblins from the likes of these? Stand and fight!"

"Ugrik's dead!" howled the terrified grey, and Klabaga clubbed him viciously to the ground.

"Come to me!" he bellowed, "I am Klabaga, Red Goblin of the Clan Modragu, and I will give you victory and the blood of human men!"

Goblins stopped their headlong flight to gather around Klabaga. Ugrik might be dead, but this was the Red Goblin who bid them come. The route slowed, and then stopped as more and more rallied to Klabaga's call. By the time the human men began their pursuit in earnest, the goblin army was no longer in retreat.

Evan galloped to the top of the Tor Mort, searching the battlefield for Klabaga. He was somewhere near. The scent of goblins and blood made his horse shy and fight the reins, but though the tapestry before him was awful and grim, a singular sight caused Evan's heart to leap with unexpected joy. Seated at the foot of the king's banner, Martin Reamon stared into space.

Aine was beside the boy before Evan could dismount. "Martin, sweet Martin," she cooed, touching his cheek, "are you much hurt?"

"Lady Aine!" he cried, and forgetting every convention he embraced her as though she were not royalty and he were not a common, awkward boy. His reaction was the same when he saw Evan, and for a time the three clung to each other and said nothing.

There on the corpse-strewn hillside they told the stories of all that had befallen them since they were parted. Each listened with wonder at the things they had overcome, and no one doubted that the Hand of Almighty God had brought them together again.

Dungal interrupted the reunion. "They're coming," he said simply. Across the meadows the human army streamed back toward the town, pursued by the resurgent goblin horde.

"To the town brave lads!" shouted Osric, knowing there was nothing else to be done. "Rally on the town." He hung his head. A few moments ago they had stood victorious against impossible

199

odds. Now they were defeated, broken, set to flight and driven toward the city where starvation and surrender awaited them.

The king was occupied with such gloomy thoughts when Evan rode up grinning as though he had done something clever. Behind him young Aine Ceallaigh, arms flung tightly about his waist, smiled as if nothing dangerous was going on around her. "What ho brother!" shouted Evan over the chaos. "Warm work, isn't it?"

Osric couldn't help but smile too. "In a day full of surprises, surely this surpasses all. What are you doing here?"

"I happened upon Lord Ceallaigh's daughter," he exclaimed, "and we decided to find out what you were doing."

"Only death is more grim than this," the king said as he watched his broken army streaming into Gwenferew. "We've come to a bad end."

Then someone called Aine's name, and her father pulled her from the horse and covered her tear-streaked face with kisses.

Time had run out. The humans took refuge in the Legion fortress, but to what eventual end, no one knew.

Already crowded, the fortress became un-manageable with the addition of the survivors from the battle. For the humans there was nothing to do but wait; wait for the final, overwhelming assault, wait for starvation, wait for death. The goblins had many options.

With Ugrik dead, Klabaga quickly and brutally secured the support of the surviving chieftains. Even Greebo couldn't deny the cunning,
skill, and leadership of the Red Goblin. He was
glamorth and the army would follow him.

For his part, Klabaga wanted control of the
goblin army for one reason; without them, Evan
MacKeth would escape. The destruction of the
town meant nothing to him now. The death of
human men was but secondary to the death of the
human boy. To obtain the desire of his heart, the
goblin army had to remain intact. He dispatched
troops to cover the approaches to the city and stationed goblins along the forest road. He wasn't
going to be surprised if another army arrived.

In Giomer's quarters the humans gathered to
find a solution to their dilemma. Everyone who
was anyone attended - Giomer and his officers, the
king and his brother, Morleigh Dunroon and Anwend Halfdane, Brendan Ceallaigh and his daughter from whom he would not suffer to be parted.
Even Isador Oxblood and Ajax the Anxious were
present, although they added nothing of value to
the conversation.

In the end they were faced with two choices:
attempt to break out of the encircled town or
tighten their belts and wait for help. Breaking out
would be problematic even for hardened soldiers,
and with women, children and the wounded in
tow, it was liable to result in massacre. Even if
they managed to force their way across the river, it
was still more than a hundred miles to Fort Cailte.
The other option assumed the Legion would even-

tually send help, though if it would be enough and if it would be in time, no one could speculate. The meeting adjourned in late afternoon without a decision. Once an accurate tally had been taken of resources and people, they would meet again.

Evan climbed to the wall walk and studied the scarred landscape. Corpses of men and goblins littered the fields of waving grass and cluttered the abandoned earthworks around the Tor Mort. Here, somehow, he would find Klabaga and kill him. Everything had fallen into place as though this had always been the plan.

Klabaga. Klabaga. Klabaga. The name pounded in his head like the thunder of goblin drums. Klabaga served the terrible spirit that had set itself against humanity. To defeat Klabaga was to defeat the spirit. In the lengthening shadows, amidst the fear and blood, their minds touched across the distance.

"Where are ya?" asked Klabaga.

"Here," Evan replied. "Waiting."

"Waiting fer what? Come out and face me human boy. Ya can't hide forever."

"Don't listen to him," said another voice. "Goblins can't be trusted. You'll meet him in God's time." Evan turned to find Julian sitting atop the battlements.

"Where have you been?" cried Evan, who to the dismay of the legionaries around him, embraced the strange creature.

"Ware! Ware!" cawed the bird. "You'll ruffle my feathers!"

"A fine Watcher you are, flying away when I most needed you! I thought you dead."

Julian shrugged. "I was *called*, just like you. I'm pleased to see you made the proper decision all on your own. There may be hope for you yet."

Evan shuddered. *The proper decision.* Had he disobeyed God, Aine would be dead. Iosa was merciful. Iosa was faithful. "Yes. The only sane choice in an insane world: trust God."

"But don't trust Klabaga. Goblins are a nasty, treacherous lot."

"So they are. But why were you *called* here?"

"It may be difficult to countenance," said Julian, beak thrust high in the air as he strutted across the palisade logs, "but there are more important things than keeping Foolish Boys out of trouble. Anyway, you'll find out soon, for good or ill. Right now, you've a visitor."

Brendan Ceallaigh appeared beside him. He bowed. "My lord," he said gravely, "may I speak with you?"

Brendan Ceallaigh being polite? What now? "Certainly," Evan replied.

"Who are you?"

It wasn't the sort of question one asked the brother of the High King. Moreover, it was a question that entailed more than it appeared to ask. After all, the Baron knew who he was. "I am he who loves your daughter."

Brendan shook his head. "That's not what I meant. Not a year ago you were a bitter, angry prisoner in my dungeon. Once lame and weak, you drove the priests from the chapel and saved my king. Now you've delivered my daughter. Who are you?"

So Evan told Brendan everything, all he had been, all he had come to be, all by the grace of Iosa Christus. "That's the answer, Baron Ceallaigh, riddle though it may seem. I love sweet Aine, but I'm God's man, a Warrior of the Son, such as I am and unworthy though I may be." Saying these things, Evan yet found them a revelation.

Brendan nodded sagely. "I don't like that bird," he said and Julian clicked defensively, "but you have my blessing to court Aine."

As if in response to the mention of her name, Aine came bounding up the stairs, excited, out of breath. "They've taken your friend," she said. "They've taken Dungal!"

"Who?"

"The Legion. They're taking him away. There!" She pointed into the press of humanity in the compound yard where Dungal towered over a knot of surrounding legionaries.

Evan pushed through the crowd, ignoring the sad, frightened faces that surrounded him. He had warned Dungal, hadn't he? He had promised to speak for the man, but now he had no faith that anyone would listen. The Legion didn't like deserters, and they didn't like anyone interfering in their business.

He intercepted them just as they were trying to shove the giant through the tiny doorway of the compound jail. It was more a large wooden box than a proper building and hadn't been constructed with someone of Dungal's stature in mind.

The big man saw Evan coming and called out. "D'ya see, there he is! Bowman . . . that is, yer grace, tell 'em I'm with you!"

"He is with me!"

The grizzled Optio in charge of the Legion detail squinted at Evan through one good eye. "That's nice. But who the devil might you be?" When informed, it made no visible impression on his demeanor.

"That's nice, *my lord*," he said, mimicking his first response, "but that don't mean nothing to me. This man's a deserter, and he'll stay in the gaol till he's tried, convicted and executed."

The Optio shouldn't have used the word *executed*, for the row that followed was as violent as it was unexpected. Dungal tossed legionaries aside like ninepins, and it took reinforcements to finally bring him down. By that time Giomer and Osric had arrived on the scene.

Evan's appeal on Dungal's behalf and Giomer's insistence that the prisoner be inserted into the guardhouse by whatever means necessary were interrupted as Braslav came bounding out of the cell. He bowled legionaries over, his eyes wild as he shoved his way through the crowd and threw himself at the feet of the king.

"Great majesty," he cried, "I bring you the means of our deliverance!"

Evan looked on bemused at the big man clutching Osric's ankles. Dungal shrugged off the remaining legionaries and braced himself in the guardhouse door. Giomer hurried to the king's aid.

"Get up you great, drunken fool!" he commanded, prodding at Braslav with the point of his sword. "Get this idiot out of here!"

Legionaries tried to dislodge him, but Braslav refused to be moved. This was his last chance, and the High King of Glenmara was the man he had to convince, if Giomer didn't kill him first.

The legionaries, unable to pry Braslav loose, began striking him with the pommels of their swords and the butts of their spears.

"Be nice father! Let the king go, can't you? You'll do yourself a mischief if you don't!"

Osric waved the legionaries away and addressed his persistent subject. "What do you want?" he scolded. "There's been enough death today, and these soldiers will kill you if you don't release me."

Braslav knew that they might very well hang him. This was the king, and he was nobody. But hanged or not, if he failed, they would all die.

"I have a message from God," he said, "and you must hear it!"

Giomer howled. "Majesty, this man is mad. He is fond of wine and hears the voices of little birds. I threw him in the guardhouse for telling such stories."

"So you speak to birds, do you?" asked Osric. "What sort of birds?"

Braslav moaned. He hadn't liked the result of this conversation before, and he was tempted to deny anything about birds of any kind, but somehow he felt that lying would be a grave mistake. Besides, it wasn't what that cursed bird said that mattered, it was what the One True God said that was important.

"Yes!" he blurted out. "I speak to birds. Not all birds mind, just this one, and it wasn't my idea! But he said things that made good sense and - there's the creature now!"

Julian landed on Evan's shoulder and hummed like a big insect.

"Get up," commanded Osric, and Braslav rose trembling before the monarch. "What is your name?"

"Braslav Tlapinski, majesty. Braslav I am."

"This is my brother, Evan Murchadha," said the king "and the bird belongs to him. It speaks to him too. What did it say to you?"

Braslav felt giddy. "It told me to seek an answer in the blood of Iosa Christus. It's a talkative thing, that persistent bird."

"And what answers did you find?"

"Everything!" Braslav enthused. "My whole life. The visions that stalk me and the death that surrounds this city."

His voice grew in intensity. "Do you think it's only those grey fellows out there? Nonsense! There's more at stake than whatever happens to us. Don't you feel it? The Lord of Shadows stalks beyond those gates. Don't fear the goblins, fear the evil of their master!"

"What rubbish!" hissed Giomer, dragging Braslav away from the king. "Shut up before you cause a panic that'll do for us all."

"Unless we pray we're done for already," cried Braslav. "We must turn our hearts to Iosa

Christus or perish!" He pulled Giomer's hands away from his tunic and turned back to the king.

"What can flesh do against the power of the Dark King whose minions howl outside these walls? Turn to Iosa, I tell you! It's the only way! Hear the word of the Lord! *Let my people call upon my name and turn to me and I will deliver them in their time of need. I shall prepare a table for them in the presence of their enemies.* Spend tonight in fasting and prayer in God's name, and with the rising of the sun we shall go forth and He will deliver the enemy into our hands. Thus sayeth the Lord God!"

A rush of excitement kindled Evan's spirit. "Your 'something to do'?" he asked Julian.

The Watcher shrugged. "I just gave him a little shove."

Braslav's oration was too much for Giomer. The idea of marching out to face the thousands of goblins infesting the plain was nothing short of suicide. "Take him," he ordered. "Get this lunatic out of here!"

But Osric waved them away. His eyes shone with understanding. It would begin here. The cleansing of his kingdom would begin tonight in Gwenferew, and in the end Glenmara would exalt the power and mercy of Iosa Christus before the entire world.

Words sprang unbidden into Braslav's mind as he addressed the crowd. "*He who dwells in the shelter of the Most High, Will abide in the shadow of the Almighty. I will say to the Lord, 'My refuge and my fortress, My God in Whom I trust!' For it is He that delivers you from the snare of the trapper and from the deadly pestilence. He will cover you with His pinions, and under His wings you may seek refuge; His faithfulness is a shield and a bulwark. You will not be afraid of the terror by night or of the arrow that flies by day, of pestilence that stalks in darkness or of the destruction that lays waste at noon. A thousand may fall at your side and ten thousand at your right hand, but it shall not approach you."*

He paused, glancing at the surrounding faces in the torchlight. He had never felt more alive or worthwhile. The Spirit of the Living God moved through him.

"Thus sayeth the God of Jacob and Moses and Abraham, the God who sent His Son to die in our place. The God of your salvation. Who will receive the gift of His mercy?"

And as the Spirit of the Lord moved among them, one by one, and Osric first of all, they fell to their knees to receive the blessing of Iosa Christus. Throughout the compound, into the far reaches of the encampment, a wave of emotion swept over the people, and they fell prostrate before the power of the Most High. Even grizzled legionaries were moved to tears, and Giomer fell silent as though fearful of calling attention to himself.

Braslav raised his hands and closed his eyes. Words sprang into his mind as though they had been hiding there all his life, only waiting for this moment to burst forth.

"Oh God, do not remain quiet, do not be silent and oh God, do not be still, For Behold, Thine

enemies make an uproar and those who hate Thee have exalted themselves. Oh my God, make them like the whirling dust, like chaff before the wind, like fire that burns the forest and like flame that sets the mountains on fire. So pursue them with Thy tempest and terrify them with Thy storm. Fill their faces with dishonor that they may seek Thy name, oh Lord. Let them be ashamed and dismayed forever and let them be humiliated and perish that they may know that Thou alone, whose name is the Lord, Art Most High over all the earth."

And the people worshipped God.

"Therefore I give you the blessing of the Lord and place you in His hands. Let no one eat or drink that you may humble yourselves, and when the sun rises we shall go forth and destroy our enemies. Thus sayeth the Lord your God whose mercy is unequaled. Amen."

It was a long while before anyone moved, reluctant to disturb the extraordinary peace that had descended upon them. The king himself at last broke the spell.

"We shall heed the words of this prophet. In the morning we shall march out to meet our enemies, and God will give us victory."

The crowd began to disperse. Osric embraced Braslav. Giomer observed Dungal on his knees, weeping like a child, and decided he could arrest him tomorrow, if anyone lived past sunrise.

Evan took Aine's hand and was filled with a fearful awe that he should love her so much. "Your father has given leave that I may court you," he said bashfully as though she might decline the opportunity. She answered by throwing her arms around him.

"Whatever comes of the morrow," she whispered, "we shall place ourselves in God's Hands, for in Him lies all our hope."

Throughout the night, others wrestled with their own emotions and the uncertainty of the day to come. Martin was overcome with a mixture of great joy at the miraculous reuniting of his master and Lady Aine and despair over the coming battle. He had never seen anything as awful as the sight and sound and smell of warfare, and he wasn't anxious for it to resume. He was trying to think of a proper prayer when Anwend Halfdane arrived with a Legion Centurion.

"Here is the boy who killed the goblin chieftain and played that little tune on the Tor Mort," the Varangian said cheerfully. "Indeed he delivered the message that brought us here to begin with. This is Centurion Einar, boy."

Martin bowed.

"Is that the sword you killed that great, ugly fellow with?" Einar asked, holding out his hand.

Martin handed over the weapon. The blade was still crusted with dried blood.

"A Legion sword," said the Centurion, "and a filthy one too. Where did you get it?"

Martin told the story of the unfortunate legionary, the message and the sword. "I never found out his name, but he asked me to tell his Centurion he did his best."

Einar nodded. "You've told me. His name was Daniel. Keep the sword, only clean it. Legion steel doesn't take kindly to rust."

Martin cleaned the sword until the blade shone like polished glass, but the prospect of using it when the sun rose was terrifying.

Morleigh Dunroon cradled dark anticipation in his heart. Standing on the wall walk, staring out across the shadowed landscape, he was eager for another chance to slay goblins. He thought it unlikely he would ever tire of killing the creatures that had murdered his mother and father.

The Legion commander faced the coming battle with pragmatic fatalism. He liked the idea of fasting since they were already desperately short of food, but the logic of that was overruled by the madness of marching out to their doom come morning. Still, he would follow orders. The king commanded it, and tomorrow Giomer would lead his men out onto the field where they would all die. It was a soldier's choice, and he found it comforting.

In the darkness beyond the Legion fortress, Klabaga called his commanders together. They consolidated their positions, sorted out units and gathered up stragglers. As soon as they were ready they would launch a final assault on the fortress, and the Red Goblin would finally come face to face with Evan MacKeth.

Yet as the night wore on, an irritating unease began to build, as though someone had lifted the curtain of night and let in the unpleasant light of broad day. In the depths of his shadowed spirit,

Klabaga sensed a growing illumination. He would be glad to kill Evan MacKeth and leave this place.

Throughout a difficult night the Red Goblin struggled with a host of problems until morning brought an unexpected solution to all of them, for as the dawn broke, the entire human army sallied from their fortress and took up positions on the plain. This was beyond good fortune or luck; it was Fate. Here on the blood-drenched fields of Clon Miarth Klabaga would begin the annihilation of all mankind. But the nagging fragment of a thought tickled at his mind, and upon this thought came the voice of Evan MacKeth.

"Are you ready?" the human boy asked unpleasantly.

"You'll see in a moment!" the goblin retorted and set his army in motion.

The human forces moved toward their foe. In the center of the line the men of the Second Legion advanced in impeccable order. But if the Legion was a model of efficiency, the muddle of humanity on either flank was shockingly chaotic. Ranks packed with unskilled merchants, old men and young boys wandered all over the field, writhing out from the stable center like headless snakes. Even the trained warriors stationed among them couldn't maintain the integrity of the line as they moved to contact with the enemy.

There was no reserve. With such a small force it was impractical to hold anything back. The tactical situation was horribly simple; they would triumph or die. Nothing else applied. On the right stood Morleigh Dunroon, Anwend Halfdane and his Varangians, on the left, Osric Murchadha, Evan MacKeth and the giant Dungal. Aine Ceallaigh accompanied the small group of archers.

It was a wholly inadequate force, less than a quarter the size of Klabaga's own. Yet beyond the fact of mere numbers, beneath the fear that hung over them like a bird of death, beneath the frailty of flesh and bone and blood, burned a faith that the One True God would save them. Silent prayer filled the morning sky.

Martin recited the same prayer over and over in a desperate singsong. "Mighty God Who can swim, save us!"

Perched on Evan's shoulder, Julian chirped and smiled. He always found comfort in prayer, even if it was funny.

Evan prayed only to do God's Will, for if events had shown him nothing else, following the Will of Iosa Christus was the only thing that made any sense and made any difference.

Osric asked God for the strength and wisdom to lead his kingdom to the worship of the One True God and drive the evil of men and goblins from his land.

Filled with an inexplicable fear, Anwend prayed a confused, plaintive prayer. The Varangian loved battle, reveled in the sweet chaos and terror of combat, so it wasn't the coming fight that weighed upon him. Rather it was because he was praying to an unfamiliar god that he found himself filled with loneliness and dread. He had always found comfort in the notion that if he fell in battle the Valkyries would bear him up to Valhalla where he would live forever with the Varangian Gods Odin, Thor and Freya. But he wasn't praying to them, one didn't pray to them, and they never answered if you did. They seemed hollow to him now, shallow, silly. So Anwend prayed to Iosa Christus in a whisper of longing and uncertainty. "Will You consider me?"

Braslav alternated between elation and tears. He knew they were doing the right thing, but the terrible spirit that hovered over the goblin army beckoned to him, taunted him. "Oh, I'm coming all right," the big man answered, wiping at the river of sweat on his brow with a filthy sleeve, "I'm coming, but you won't like Who I'm bringing with me!"

And on they came, steadily, inexorably toward the goblin army awaiting them on the meadows of Clon Miarth. Klabaga was content to let them come.

Giomer drove straight for the center of the goblin line, hoping to punch through and cause as much havoc as possible. He knew, despite the fervent prayer, the fasting and all the other foolishness, that they would soon be dead, so he approached the hopelessness as though it were a training exercise.

His legionaries wore their parade finery, best embroidered tunics, bronze polished to a brilliant luster and helmets bedecked with garish plumes. One might as soon die looking the proper soldier. Centurions herded their men like mother hens, keeping exact cover and alignment and in hovering over such details, succeeded in dulling the edge of fear. They were afraid, but they were legionaries and would do their duty.

Giomer had never seen an attack pressed home with such precision. Javelins arched up like a flight of iron birds and came down among the goblins in a hail of destruction. The first rank closed with the enemy while more spears from those legionaries behind impacted the opposing ranks. Such was the perfect violence of that first charge that they broke through Klabaga's center. The Legion poured through the gap only to be stopped by a second, stronger goblin line, and the legionaries found themselves surrounded and cut off from the rest of the army.

Now Klabaga set the rest of his forces in motion on the right and left, and the human army, split apart at its center was hurled staggering back. The goblins rolled up their flanks, cutting them off from the city.

No more than ten minutes had passed since the fighting commenced and already the humans were being pushed from the field, their army scattered and fighting desperately just to stay alive. They fell back toward the abandoned goblin earthworks in two disorganized masses, each threatened with envelopment by the grey tides swirling around them. But if the humans were now split into three distinct groups, the goblins were likewise divided.

Osric's men, fighting furiously, managed to reach the Tor Mort where they were quickly surrounded. Yet here they managed to repulse the goblin assault.

Out on the plain, Morleigh Dunroon's forces were thrust back against the city walls by the inexorable tide of goblins. Trapped, impossibly beset from every quarter, they tried to account themselves well, though their numbers grew smaller at every stroke of goblin steel. Yet while despair began to overwhelm the hearts of everyone else, Braslav grew wild with an unquenchable anger.

He sensed the Great Shadow hovering over them, mocking their efforts, their faith. He shook his cutlass at the sky. "Have You not promised us this day? Have we not obeyed Your command? Who are these creatures that would defy Your Will, Oh Mighty Lord?"

He struck down one goblin, then another and a third and called out to those men yet standing.

"Do you not know the faithfulness of Iosa Christus? He has given us victory and nothing may stand before His might! Strike! Strike! Deus Vult! Gods Wills it!" Braslav became a terror before which the goblins gave way. But there were still so many.

Locked in a wall of shields, the Legion braced itself against the frenzy of the goblin attack. "Hold!" Giomer cried. "Steady on! An extra ration of beer to whoever lives out the day!" The legionaries laughed and did their best to hold their formation together. No one believed they would taste beer again.

Sensing Evan MacKeth nearby became too much for Klabaga to ignore. He left Greebo in charge of destroying the Legion and turned toward his enemy.

He found him on the Tor Mort. When their eyes met, Klabaga knew this was the same insignificant boy that had killed so many goblins in Westerfeld and who, against reason, had destroyed the Glamorth. The unease Klabaga had felt the night before peaked, filling his mind with images of bonfires stretching across a barren, treeless plain, flames devouring countless goblin corpses. He saw ruin, defeat, destruction and the end to the ambitions of his race.

Visions rose around Evan too as he gazed into the pale yellow eyes of the Red Goblin, the promise of misery and horror that Klabaga would bring to the world of men. As long as the goblin lived that promise would hang over mankind like a curse. This was the reason Evan was here: to stand against the darkness that came in Klabaga's wake. Evan cried out, and Klabaga answered his challenge.

Evan launched himself at the goblin line with such ferocity that he was suddenly deep among them. Julian clawed, bit, and spouted flame while Dungal battered his way through to reach Evan's side. The humans pushed through the gap, splitting the goblin formation in two.

The frantic fight quickly degenerated into a chaos of disordered carnage. Formations split apart, disintegrated into hundreds of smaller struggles, and spilled over the hillside onto the plain beyond. Amidst the confusion, Evan found Klabaga.

They went at each other like animals, swords striking sparks as they whirled past. Evan turned on his heel and delivered a backhand slash to take Klabaga from behind, but such was the speed and agility of the Red Goblin that Evan cut only empty air and barely managed to parry a strike aimed at his head. As it was his hand stung from the power of Klabaga's blow.

He lunged, feinted low and reversed his wrist to strike high, but Klabaga danced back and slashed down as Evan's attack came up short, and the boy had to throw himself to the ground to stay alive. Evan cut at Klabaga's legs, leapt to his feet, and then the pair closed with each other in a mad rush.

Klabaga was larger, more powerful than the human boy, and as they came together it was Evan who was lifted up and thrown violently down. Yet drawing on all his skill, he threw his weight to one side so that the Red Goblin landed beside him, not atop, as they impacted the ground. The goblin's sword glanced off Evan's shirt of Legion maille, and Evan's own blade deflected from Klabaga's armor as they struggled to their feet.

Klabaga struck at Evan's shoulder but turned the blade at the last moment, bringing it across his opponent's legs. Partially blocked, it was still enough to open a nasty cut above the boy's knee. Evan's hasty lunge sank into Klabaga's muscled forearm.

They circled, snarling, searching for an opening, an advantage, a weakness. Around them two opposing armies tore themselves to bits, but they took no notice as though they weren't part of the broader struggle.

Again they closed, grappling, twisting, battering at each other, screaming and cursing, biting and tearing in a savage embrace. Evan felt the goblin's evil power and sought with all his might to destroy him. Klabaga sensed in his opponent a force beyond mere physical prowess, and he knew he would never face a more dangerous foe.

Still, Glandahoo had trained him well, and Klabaga had already learned much about the way the boy fought. The human was fast and agile, but he couldn't match Klabaga in strength, so the Red Goblin bore down upon him with all the brutal force he could muster. Like hammers ringing in a madman's forge, their swords glanced from each other in a savage symphony of steel. Evan fell back before the remorseless attack.

Klabaga gloried in the moment as he battered his foe with blows that if landed couldn't fail to kill. Evan dodged and gave way, parrying only when there was no other choice, for with each jarring impact of Klabaga's blade upon his own, his grip weakened and his strength diminished.

But for all his power, Klabaga's muscles were but flesh, and mere blood coursed through his veins. He gasped for breath. His blows became clumsy. The Red Goblin stumbled.

Seeing Klabaga falter, Evan lunged, but the goblin parried and closed yet again. Klabaga hurled the boy down, gouged, bit and battered at him with broad fists. They cast aside swords and went at each other like wild beasts, struggling among the growing heaps of wounded and dead from the battle that raged about them.

Atop the Tor Mort, Aine Ceallaigh marked targets in the mad swirl of combat below. As she sent arrow after arrow into the seething mass of grey flesh, she wept, for her beloved had been engulfed by that angry sea. Her father was out there too, and Osric and Martin, and she despaired of seeing any of them again. The human army could not stand against such numbers. Still, as she reached into her dwindling supply of arrows, her faith remained in Iosa's mercy.

Martin found himself at the base of the Tor, pushed against a mound of dead goblins and men twisted together in a grisly puzzle of mangled flesh. Here he stood with a handful of others and fought to stay alive.

Dungal did his best to keep the tide from overwhelming Evan. He set his feet wide apart, gripped his sword in both hands, and lay about like an unbalanced windmill. He had been in some dreadful fights before, brutal, nasty affairs, but nothing approaching this, and he wondered if he had made a mistake by not listening to Bran. He hoped Bran had gotten away.

Bran had not gotten away. He and his men crouched among the trees at the very edge of the forest and watched the battle unfold. The big man scratched at his beard and spat in disgust. All those fools out there would be dead before the sun reached its zenith, and he wanted to be far away by then. He would have already been far away but for the goblins that always seemed to be where he was trying to go. Since parting with Dungal, he and his little band had made several unsuccessful attempts to break through to the west. Now with the goblins busy slaughtering the soldiers of the king, they had another chance to escape. On top of this, they had stumbled across an unexpected treasure. There in the wood, still tethered to the trees, were the horses of Osric's army.

Of course, stealing five hundred horses complete with harness and accoutrements was a certain way to end up on the short end of a rope, but the previous owners wouldn't survive the day. The money to be made from the saddles alone was staggering. Bran began to believe his luck had turned at last.

They herded their plunder together and drove west toward the narrow trail that would take them to safety and a rich future. Bran cast a final glance at the Legion banner in the meadow.

The Legion faltered. There were too many goblins, and Giomer knew that prayers couldn't overcome simple arithmetic. He had known it from the beginning and it came as no surprise that in a few moments they would all be dead. Still, it was how he would have wished to die, with the cloying smell of blood assailing his nostrils, the sweet and terrible sound of battle pounding a drumbeat in his ears like a mad waltz. It was the proper way for a legionary to go, a quick and violent end in the prime of manhood rather than lingering into old age, crippled, diseased, and eking out a meager living on a Legion pension. But Giomer grieved for every man who fell around him, his children that he had so wanted to save.

The ring of bright red Legion shields grew smaller and smaller.

Pushed back to the city walls, Morleigh Dunroon rallied his men behind Braslav. Were this a normal moment, Braslav would have long ago collapsed from exhaustion. He wasn't fit and though his great size gave him a certain attendant strength, he should have been wheezing for breath by now. Instead, with each blow from his cutlass, his strength redoubled, with each goblin slain his spirit soared, for the harder he fought the more the evil spirit recoiled.

At first it was almost indiscernible, as though the great, hovering shadow had merely rippled in the breeze. But as Braslav called out for the goblins to submit to Iosa Christus, the terror that had always stalked him began to withdraw. As it withdrew, Braslav advanced.

Goblins advanced up the Tor Mort. The archers met them with a stinging hail of arrows that felled many but failed to stop their rush. One more volley and the goblins were among them.

The defenders scattered before the goblin attack. Martin looked up in time to see Aine, feet braced wide apart, swinging a ponderous axe in a clumsy arch. With a clarity that brought the horror of the day to a distinct focus, Martin watched helplessly as a goblin struck Aine Ceallaigh down. She collapsed as though she had never been alive.

"No!" Martin screamed, but his voice was lost in the cacophony of battle.

The boy clawed his way over the barricade of dead. Slipping in the unspeakable carnage covering the slope he struggled to the spot where Aine Ceallaigh lay. The goblin leaned over her, pawing at her body, and with a strength heightened by rage, Martin stabbed once, twice, three times until his sword wedged in the dying creature and was pulled from his hand as it fell. Wrestling the body aside he cradled Aine in his arms.

"*Surely the sky cannot be so blue if she is dead,*" he thought. "*Surely the world will crash into ruin if she is slain!*"

All around him the world appeared to be crashing into ruin as the goblins cut the human army to pieces.

Evan MacKeth and Klabaga of the Clan Modragu were tearing each other to pieces too. It was a fight beyond savagery, beyond brutality, degenerated into a contest of brute animal strength that knew neither pity nor remorse. Clawing, strangling, kicking and biting, they sought to destroy one another.

Klabaga kicked Evan away and snatched up his sword. Evan retrieved his own weapon, parried, sidestepped and cut a bloody furrow beneath the goblin's chin. The dance of steel continued unabated. But like the slaughter around them, it couldn't last forever. The end was near.

Bran could see the end too. The battle was behind them, the noise entirely blotted out by the thunder of hooves as they herded the horses west. Within a few miles the forest road would disgorge them onto a broad plain and the way to Dhub would be open. Bran smiled. He had managed to get out of another tight spot. He began to whistle a happy tune from his youth.

"Goblins! Goblins!" warned one of the bandits.

The forest erupted with grey shapes. Already nervous from the smell of goblins and blood, the horses panicked, and in an instant the entire herd swept back up the road toward Clon Miarth, taking Bran Mael Morda and his bandits with them. They careened up the roadway and spread out in an irresistible tide across the battlefield.

The earth trembled from the violent rhythm of thousands of iron-shod hooves. Goblin formations poised to annihilate what remained of the Legion detachment were scattered in fragments as the stampede slammed into them. The Legion shield wall broke apart with a sound like an avalanche as the horses crashed through, throwing down goblin and human alike.

Seconds later the stampede crested the ridgeline and burst upon Braslav's steady advance. This struggle too was smashed into tatters as everyone fled for their lives. The horses turned south, up and over the ruined goblin earthworks and bore down upon the chaotic tangle on the Tor Mort.

Battered and bloody, Evan swung at Klabaga's head, missed and went down. Klabaga brought his sword down with arms that trembled from the strain of prolonged combat and missed his target by inches. Evan rolled away, struggled to regain his feet, staggered, and fell. Klabaga loomed above, poised to strike and then paused, looking away. The ground rumbled as though the world was trying to shake itself to pieces. Evan stabbed upward, felt the blade sink into Klabaga's flesh, and then the horses came upon them like the end of the world. Darkness followed.

———————

The battle was over. Thousands of goblins, streamed westward toward the mountains and the safety of their sunless caverns. Thousands more lay dead or wounded beneath the canopy of brilliant blue sky. Humans too, lifeless or injured, littered the ravaged landscape. Others wandered about like lost children.

The tattered remnant of the Gwenferew Legion stood in formation on the spot they had shed so much blood to hold. Of the five hundred legionaries that had garrisoned the town, less than fifty remained fit for duty and all were wounded. As many more wouldn't live to see another day. Giomer Lorich surveyed the carnage and choked back tears that so many of his brave boys had fallen, but he had never been more proud to be a legionary.

He swayed on his feet, and Ronan hurried to his side. "The surgeon is coming Domini," offered the Tribune, "and we've sent a detail to fetch water. Won't you sit down sir?"

Giomer shook his head, but not in answer to the question. He was overawed by what had happened right before his eyes. A handful of legionaries with a handful of rabble and a handful of horses had smashed the goblin army. Hadn't that drunken fool Braslav said they would do it? He wondered if the unfortunate fellow had survived the outcome.

Indeed, Braslav was very much alive. He sat on a big rock out in the meadow, wiping the sweat from his brow and mumbling to himself.

"Didn't You tell them? Of course You did! There's no power like Yours. That evil spirit is gone right enough. Oh, not destroyed, but didn't I see it running away with all those goblins? Running like a frightened rabbit! I thank You Mighty Lord, for Your Deliverance. I am Your man now. I serve only You, for You have rescued me from the Shadow."

Survivors gathered about him. "Pray for us," they insisted. "Let us give thanks to the One True God."

So Braslav stood on the rock and prayed a prayer of thanksgiving and worship and the people prayed with him. Morleigh Dunroon fell to his knees, raised his notched sword toward heaven and swore fealty to Iosa Christus. Anwend Half-dane knelt beside him, not knowing what to say, though his heart was so full.

A dull, terrible rattle replaced the sharp sound of battle. The dying called for water, for wives, sweethearts and mothers. Some begged for a final end to their torment. Goblins too, abandoned on the bloody meadow, cried out, but the victors had no mercy for them.

Martin gently brushed Aine's blood matted hair from her eyes. How could he tell his master that she was dead? Was his master even alive?

"God," he cried out, "You rescued me from the river. You led me to the message that brought us to this place of death. Don't take her. Take me! What good am I to anyone? I can't bear to live if she must die!"

The One True God answered.

"Oh Martin," whispered Aine, "how you do carry on."

Osric Murchadha gathered his retainers and tried to forge order from chaos. The stampede that saved them had done its share of damage among the victors. But the field was theirs, the goblins were fled into the mountains, and the city, at least for the present, had been spared.

Nearby, Evan stirred from a comforting nothingness to the painful annoyance of something repeatedly thrusting against his chest. Julian continued to peck away. "Begone Wretched Bird," demanded Evan, "ere you do me a mischief."

The Watcher smiled and clicked. "Then get up lazy boy. The battle is won!"

Evan struggled upright, grimacing from the pain of his wounds and the results of being trampled by horses. "Klabaga?" he asked, looking around for the body of the Red Goblin.

"Gone. Fled along with the rest of his brood. He was wounded."

Evan shook his head in disappointment. "I cannot rest and him still alive. He must die."

"Another day," counseled Julian, "There will be another day."

The same thought filled Klabaga's mind as he made his way into the mountains with the remnant of the goblin host. Horses had done for them this time. Next time it would be different. Next time there would be a reckoning, and Evan MacKeth would die. With a final backward glance and a silent curse for the human boy, he disappeared beneath the earth.

Evan turned toward the distant mountains and spied Bran Mael Morda sitting on the ground nearby. "What are you doing here? I thought you'd gone."

Bran cursed and spat. "Don't talk to me!" he snarled, "It was a dark day when I met you, and the sun hasn't risen since!"

With animated venom Bran told a tale of stolen horses, a sudden, terrifying stampede and being thrown from his own mount.

"Your thievery has saved us!" laughed Evan.

"It hasn't saved everyone," retorted Bran. "There lies Dungal."

Dungal lay amidst a tangle of dead goblins, and though he was still breathing, Evan couldn't imagine what was keeping the big man alive. A vicious wound across his chest revealed the white of bone. The boy knelt with a certain reverence. "Brave heart," he said, taking Dungal's hand, "I've never fought a harder man than you."

"What about that red fellow?" whispered Dungal. "Weren't he hard too?"

"Not like you. Never like you."

"Did ya kill him?"

Evan shook his head.

"You're supposed to, ain't it? Yer'll find him and finish the job. Ya will, bowman."

He spoke as though he sensed the tie between Evan and the Red Goblin, but there was something else in the dim light of his eyes. He squeezed Evan's hand.

"I prayed ta yer God," he said.

"Don't waste your strength," interrupted Bran. "Be quiet now like a good lad."

"No Bran. This is important."

He paused, trying to rally enough strength to continue. "I didn't know what to say to yer God. I prayed, but what if I used the wrong words?"

"He heard you," assured Evan with a smile.

"But I want what you've got, young laird. He talks to ya, don't He? His power runs in yer blood. I'd like to see Him, this God of yours."

Bran hissed in Evan's ear. "I don't care if you're the King's brother. Don't fill his simple head with a lot of nonsense!"

Evan ignored the warning. "You'll see Him Dungal. I'll pray with you."

Evan said the words and Dungal carefully repeated them. When the simple prayer of repentance was done, Dungal squeezed Evan's hand, closed his eyes and stopped breathing.

Bran spat. "Well that tops it all, doesn't it? You killed him from telling lies, and the last words he hears from your lips are lies! Lies! If your God had any power you wouldn't have been slaughtered like so many sheep!"

"My God used an ill-tempered bandit and a herd of horses to save us. My God knows you, Bran Mael Morda, and He loves you."

"I don't want him to love me!" Bran said, gesturing at the carnage covering the meadow. "Look what He does to those He 'loves.' I just want Him to leave me alone!"

Dungal cried out and his eyes flew open. The grip on Evan's hand was strong.

"Will ya look at that!" he said in wonderment. "I see Him. It's that Iosa fellow. He's calling my name. My name! Oh Bowman, you were right!"

He laughed, tears streaming down his pale face. "I'm coming sweet Lamb! Goodbye Bowman, goodbye Bran. I'm going home."

And so Dungal went to be with his Savior.

Bran looked on bewildered. Something had just happened, but the meaning eluded him. Delusion? Madness born of pain? He didn't really want to know.

"Behold the power of my God," said Evan, "and witness His everlasting mercy."

"Power? Mercy? You're a fool!" railed Bran, but there was a trembling fearfulness in his voice. "The man's dead. Where's the power and mercy in that?"

"You're the fool, Bran Mael Morda, to disbelieve the evidence of your own eyes. But you will know. The Hand of God is upon you, and you cannot escape. Hide if you like, run, deny, try to drown out His voice with hatred and despair. I did. But in the end He will still be there, calling your name."

Bran leveled his sword at Evan's chest. "You're mad. Mad! Stay away from me Bowman. Next I see you I'll gut you like a fish. D'ya hear?"

He turned sharply and disappeared among the shallow hills.

Julian lit on Evan's shoulder and gestured with a wing. "Look there."

Martin struggled to carry Aine down the face of the Tor Mort.

"Sweet girl," Evan said, taking her from Martin and kissing her dirty cheek, "you've done yourself a mischief."

She smiled and nuzzled her head against Evan's chest. "Did we win?"

"We won," Evan replied.

"A glorious victory," said the Watcher.

———————

It was indeed a glorious victory, yet even glorious victories are filled with their share of mourning and despair. Thousands were dead. Many more had been dragged in chains beneath the mountain. Families searched for missing loved ones and for every miraculous reunion there were hundreds who fruitlessly searched on. Many of the wounded died in spite of all that could be done. Of the Varangians who had followed Anwend Halfdane halfway across the world to these bitter meadows, only five had survived. One of these was Ragnar, who against hope, was discovered alive amongst the dead on the Tor Mort.

From the aftermath of battle Osric, Giomer and Morleigh organized the survivors into a ragged army, less than two hundred men fit to bear arms, comprised of knights and nobles, peasants and merchants, legionaries and militiamen. Despite differences in training and social class, having shared the experience of the battle, they were as brothers.

Late in the afternoon of the following day, a relief column of six hundred legionaries from Fort Cailte arrived in Gwenferew. They were received with dull enthusiasm. Had they arrived a day earlier many lives might have been saved, yet the provisions they brought prevented further suffering.

Gwenferew was saved, but the future was full of gathering clouds. Rebellious Dukes threatened civil war, and somewhere in the darkness beneath the world the Red Goblin searched for the power that could defeat the followers of the Light.

EPILOGUE

Evan reined his horse in atop the high mountain pass where the road descended into Ondria. Behind him, Glenmara was lost in a swirling haze of snow-heavy clouds.

The youth pulled his cloak tighter as the wind howled among the trees and rocks. On his shoulder the Watcher shivered and longed for the warmth of summers past. Snow stood deep on the ground even though it was early September. While sensible people huddled around the warmth of hearth and home, Evan MacKeth traveled west to Xulanct and the dark city of Nezadsahr.

He dwelt neither on the brewing winter storm nor his distant destination. Rather his thoughts turned to Durham and all he had left behind. So much had happened in the few short months since the battle of Gwenferew that it seemed time was spinning out of control. Without proper explanation or adequate preparation, Evan found himself in this cold, lonely pass, high in the Iarlaithe Mountains.

Within days of the victory over the goblins, Osric departed for Durham with the remnant of his army. The Legion rebuilt the town walls, dismantled the goblin siege works and toiled for days burying or burning the dead. It was some while before Spring breezes carried pleasant odors through the streets of Gwenferew.

Evan stayed with Aine until she was well enough to travel. The goblin sword had left a nasty gash across the side of her head, and though the Legion surgeon remained confident of her recovery, she suffered from terrible headaches for some time to come.

Elsewhere throughout the kingdom Osric marshaled his vassals, consolidated his power and secured his holdings. In a battle against the forces of Duke Laighan, the king found himself beset by a second hostile army under Duke Ringan. At great cost, the king managed to disengage and fall back to Durham.

The leaves turned and fell, and were scattered by the cold winds. Winter put a temporary halt to the bloodshed.

Aine remained in Durham, cared for by Ivrian, doted upon by Brendan, worried over by Martin. Evan set about courting her in proper Glenmaran fashion. Placed in the hands of the One True God, their love grew stronger.

Brian Beollan returned to Durham. The devastation attendant with seeing Aine and Evan together was overpowered by the joy of seeing Aine safe. Though he couldn't rejoice that his sweetheart loved another, he contented himself with the miracle of her deliverance.

Martin attended his master and Lady Aine and watched discreetly as they acted like fools around each other. Then, to his great surprise, he was summoned before the king and knighted for services to the crown. Showered with armor and weapons, he was given the fief of a fallen knight. Anwend even paid him the promised gold for the goblin banner.

Snow came early, but Evan and Aine scarcely noticed the cold. They found warmth enough in their love and the excitement of youth. But in the dark of a long winter night, an evil disturbing dream came to Evan, filled with portents and possibilities. Once again he had been *called*.

Though his heart was heavy at the thought of leaving his sweetheart, there was no question about his going. His life was pledged to Iosa Christus. But would Aine understand?

Aine understood. Her love wasn't like other men, and his life was not his own. She wanted him to stay, but how could they deny the will of God?

So Aine stayed, and Evan went and there was no joy in any of it. There was only the deep, troubling knowledge that events were in motion that would change the entire world and anything done or left undone would have a drastic effect on the whole.

The world continued around them, but the lovers took no notice. Little time remained, and they treated each moment together as their last. They pledged their love in dozens of ways, exchanging little gifts as though this trinket or that could preserve their affection and devotion across the miles and perhaps the years.

Evan left one winter morning in the midst of a slow, heavy snowfall. From a tower rising high above the Sceir Naid, Aine watched him go. It was in God's hands now, as it had been from the beginning. Man's plots and schemes ended with an emptiness only God could fill. There was no mercy in man save through God and there was no future for man but through that mercy. Yet it was hard to think of such things with a broken heart, when everything you loved was being left behind or was going away.

Evan's path took him first to the little village of O'Byrne. It remained exactly as he remembered, the fields, though now covered in snow, the stream, though now frozen, the surrounding forests, though now bare and covered with ice. Smoke from chimneys hung low across the valley as it always had, and the dour fortress that had once belonged to his mother still stood lonely guard over the collection of crude huts that made up the town.

His horse clattered across the bridge, past the dark, foreboding mill where in another life he had nearly perished at the hands of a mud troll. At the wooden-walled castle, soldiers challenged Evan, but their suspicion changed to respectful glee at the return of their young lord. The bell atop the keep rang out, and the villagers gathered to pay respect to their liege. Evan returned their gracious enthusiasm, but a hollow ache weighed upon his heart as memories rose around him.

In the morning he rode into the forest, stopping at a familiar glade. For a long while he sat in the cold beneath a great tree, his eyes closed as he let the past overwhelm the present and future.

Whack! "Keep your guard up, young laird or you'll lose your fingers!" Julian Antony Vorenius warned.

"Haven't I already?" howled the boy.

"Not yet, but it's still early."

Evan smiled as the panorama of memories swept over him like a warm wind. "One day I'll find you, Julian. One day."

Before he left O'Byrne he summoned the Warden, gave him a handful of coins and bid him find a stone carver. In the spring, the little glade would boast a marble cross in remembrance of Iosa's sacrifice and the man who had revealed the truth to a spoiled, selfish boy. There would even be an inscription: *Is dies pro Senior!*

Now he looked back on Glenmara for what might be the last time. Yet even so, he felt a certain excitement. Behind him lay everything he loved, but before him lay a world filled with desperate adventure. What young warrior wouldn't rejoice at that?

Evan yelped as Julian bit his arm. "That hurt!"

"Of course!" replied the Watcher. "Don't you recall when you languished in the palace, filled with self-pity and despair? A very sage bird told you that everything would turn out for the best. That same remarkable creature promised to bite you one day to remind you of his wisdom. I keep promises."

Evan rubbed his arm. "You are remarkable - remarkably obnoxious. But I'll accept your worth if only to keep you from reminding me again."

"Foolish Boys need reminding."

"And Wretched Birds must mind their manners."

"That's Zalathrax to you!"

Evan reined his horse west. "No such thing as a Zalathrax," he said, and the Warrior of the Son and his Watcher began the long journey to Nezadsahr.

(Continued in *Fire From the Earth*)

GLOSSARY

A brief list of pronunciation

NAME	PRONUNCIATION
Aine Ceallaigh	Ayn Kelly
Ascalon	Askálon
Augustus Claes	Augustus Clays
Balinora Mountains	Balinóra Mountains
Bran Mael Morda	Bran Maal Morda
Claranides	Clara nighdeeze
Dungal	Doongall
Durham	Doórum
Eonacht	Yaánok
Evan MacKeth	Evun Mukéth
Faltigern	Faáltigurn
Glamorth	Glamórth
Glenmara	Glenmaára
Glenne	Glen
Iarlaithe	Eeárleth
Illyria	Illiŕia
Iosa Christus	Yosa Christoos
Ivrian Ceallaigh	Ivrian Kelly
Julian Vorenius	Julian Voréneeus
Kevin Mac Maoilorian	Kevin Mac Mailórian
Klabaga	Klabaága
Moloch	Mahlock
Nezadsahr	Nézoddsaar

The Fields of Clon Miarth

O'Byrne	O' Burn
Osric Murchadha	Ozric Mur-kaáda
Pelakapar	Pelaćupar
River Aiden	River Aíden
River Cuinn	River Shawn
River Gabhailin	River Gabáylin
River Orth	River Orth
Xulanct	Zoolánkt